*Suddenly He Pulled Her Into the
Loving Shelter of His Arms*

and Nicola felt a languor steal over her
body that she'd never known before. He
bent down and kissed her thoroughly and
possessively on the lips. Then he was
kissing the hollow of her throat, while his
hands moved over her, gently, surely.
And when he started to kiss her again,
Nicola's heartbeat thundered like a
coastal storm as she felt herself caught up
in a happiness beyond all her dreams. . . .

TO CATCH
A BRIDE

by Glenna Finley

A SIGNET BOOK

NEW AMERICAN LIBRARY

TIMES MIRROR

SIGNET, SIGNET CLASSICS, MENTOR, PLUME AND MERIDIAN BOOKS
are published by The New American Library, Inc.,
1301 Avenue of the Americas, New York, New York 10019

FIRST PRINTING, NOVEMBER, 1977

1 2 3 4 5 6 7 8 9

PRINTED IN THE UNITED STATES OF AMERICA

She whom I love is hard to catch
and conquer,
Hard, but O the glory of the winning
were she won!

—GEORGE MEREDITH

1

Nicola Warren was still happily unaware of what the fates had in store for her when she swung off a Madison Avenue bus that sunny Monday morning in early October and started down Seventy-second Street.

She had lived in Manhattan for three years, long enough not to be surprised by anything she encountered on the sidewalk—whether it was attached to a leash or just jogging by. Nevertheless she did smile as an overweight man in a warm-up suit loped past with a miniature poodle trotting resignedly at his side. When the dog would have detoured to a fire hydrant, his owner gave him a sharp command and the poodle guiltily hurried to catch up.

Nicola stared over her shoulder at them and smiled in a way that made a passing cabdriver forget the miniscule tip his last fare had bestowed. The traffic light at the corner turned red, so the cabbie had a little longer to admire her shoulder-length blonde hair and trim size-ten figure evident under a scarlet topcoat. His glance had just moved down to approve an admirable pair of ankles when the driver in the car behind him impatiently blasted his horn. That maneuver brought about the conventional response; the cabbie shot his head out of his car window screaming about the inept and mentally deficient human beings found behind a steering wheel these days.

Nicola ignored the furore and walked on to the ground-floor entrance of a townhouse in the middle of the block, serenely unaware that she was responsible for the shouting match at the corner, which was then attracting a policeman as referee.

She unlocked a dark green door with a gleaming brass knocker and passed into the tranquillity of another world—the spacious slate foyer furnished with tasteful leather furniture which functioned as a reception room for Alex Laird's photographic enterprises. Nicola thought once again that her employer should be given full marks for his remodeling project, which transformed the staff quarters of an elegant, but ancient townhouse into convenient offices and studios for his busy commercial and high-fashion accounts.

As she moved over to put her purse on her desk in the first room off the foyer, she glanced instinctively toward the connecting door at the side of it, which led to Alex's office. That morning the premises were unnaturally quiet, since the lord and master had flown to Mexico City on an assignment the week before and had given his two darkroom helpers the time off. Only Nicola, who served as his secretary and general factotum, was expected to remain on duty in the studio during his absence.

A buzzer sounded at her elbow, and she flipped a switch. "Good morning, William," she said into the intercom. "Beautiful morning, isn't it?"

"Very nice, Miss Nicola." The elderly man who ran Alex's domestic household in the townhouse above sounded preoccupied. "Mr. Alex wants you to call him as soon as possible. Apparently he tried to reach you at home."

"I was away in Connecticut for the weekend. . . ."

"That's what I told him, Miss Nicola."

Good for William, Nicola thought. There was an unspoken pact between them, since their employer was addicted to twelve-hour days on his work schedule and expected his houseman and secretary to follow his lead. Nicola found that it was no use trying to change his mind, as Alex wasn't at all reluctant to pay for her overtime services; he simply wanted her at his beck and call seven days a week. There was nothing personal in his attitude; Nicola was expected to keep his appointments straight and his checkbook in immaculate condition. Someday he'd discover that she could be replaced by a computer, and she'd be sent on her way with a cool handshake and his best wishes.

"There's a number in Mexico City that you're to call," William said, interrupting her unhappy soliloquy. "I'll send it down with the coffee."

"All right . . . and thank you, William. The coffee will be welcome; I had to catch an early train back to town. Did Mr. Laird say when he was coming back?"

There was a slight pause then. "I'm not sure. The connection wasn't very good. You'd better ask him."

If she hadn't known better, Nicola could have sworn that the old gentleman was being evasive. She bit her lip thoughtfully as he said, "I'll put the coffee on the trolley now," and heard the click as he switched off.

Her expression was still pensive as she went through the studio area into their mini-kitchen, waiting until the dumbwaiter clicked into place. To William, coffee was always sent down on the trolley—any other term for the mechanism was beneath his dignity. Just the way that the houseman's thirty-five years of domestic service with the Laird family made him ignore Alex's photographic ventures. Nicola had a suspicion that Alex's personal life on the floors above conformed to William's rigid rules. She'd often wondered what the old retainer thought about the models that Alex dated from time to time— usually gorgeous thin creatures who were delighted to be escorted by the man whose professional talents made them look even better. It didn't hurt that he was a ruggedly good-looking bachelor in his early thirties with an impressive family background.

Nicola shook her head as she opened the dumbwaiter and took out an immaculate coffee tray. No Styrofoam mugs for William, she thought happily as she carried the tray to her desk. She poured a cup of steaming liquid before picking up the piece of paper with Alex's telephone number on it. Sitting down in her desk chair, she took a sip of coffee for reassurance and then put the call through. Alex didn't make a habit of leaving urgent messages; something must have happened to upset his plans.

There was a brief period of static on the wire and a couple of minor explosions in the receiver before she was connected with the hotel in Mexico City and an operator who was reluctant to abandon Spanish for halting English. Then there was another wait while the reception clerk tried to sort out the proper room number for Señor Laird. Finally she heard the sound of a receiver being lifted and an impatient masculine voice saying, "Hullo. Nicola . . . is that you?" At the same time, the hotel operator announced that there was a long-distance call from New York for Señor Laird. "Yes, yes, I understand, thanks," he said, cutting her off decisively. "Nicola . . . can you hear me?"

"Loud and clear," she murmured, forgetting her proper role for a minute.

"What's that?"

She recovered quickly. "I can hear you very well, Mr. Laird. William said you wanted me to call."

"I certainly did. Where the hell have you been?"

"What do you mean?" Her voice squeaked with indignation. "I'm early. It's only"—she put down her coffee cup to check the watch on her wrist—"ten to eight here."

"I didn't ask you what time it was. I've been trying to reach you ever since last night."

"I spent the weekend in Connecticut. . . ."

"So William said. Next time, leave a number with somebody, for God's sake."

Nicola was inclined to argue. She wanted to say that she was simply a private secretary, not one of the doctors Mayo, and therefore, if she wanted to spend a relaxing Sunday in Connecticut, it wasn't a federal crime. There was a considerable pause while she thought about all those things. Then she remembered that the irritable man at the other end of the wire signed a very generous paycheck, so she swallowed her anger. "I'll do that," she promised quietly. "I'm sorry you were inconvenienced. Did you want me for something special, Mr. Laird?"

Strangely enough, her courtesy didn't mollify him. If anything, he sounded even angrier than before when he snapped, "I'm not calling you just to improve Pan-American relations. I'm going to have to change my schedule for the next couple of weeks."

"Oh?" Her voice remained carefully polite. "Do you want me to rearrange your shooting appointments?"

"I want you to cancel them . . . that's what I'm trying to get across. I can't go back to work before the end of the month . . . that's the earliest date the damned doctor will promise."

"Doctor? Alex! For heaven's sake, what's wrong with you?" Nicola's formality disappeared in her agitation.

Evidently he didn't notice her slip. "It's not a session of Montezuma's revenge—if you're trying to be tactful. I twisted my ankle yesterday on some cobblestones when I was trying to get a decent shot of that gate at Chapultepec Castle. You know the one."

Nicola nodded and then realized the futility of the gesture. "Yes, I remember," she said. "Is it hurt badly—your ankle, I mean?"

"I didn't *think* you were talking about the wrought-iron fence. My foot hurts like hell, but I've been told in fluent Spanish that I'll live."

"It might be nice if you heard it in fluent English."

"I know. That's what I thought." There was a tired undertone to his voice that she hadn't noticed before. "So I made a reservation on the noon plane to Los Angeles. I can pick up a connecting flight to San Diego without any trouble. Juliette has arranged a sublet in a condominium there . . . she says the sunshine will do us good."

Nicola's spirits plunged to her shoetops. "Us? You mean . . . you and Juliette?" She hadn't known that Alex had that kind of relationship with the brunette model he'd been photographing on the Mexican assignment.

"Of course not." Alex's denial sounded heavenly in her ears. "I'm talking about you and me. Unless my discreet Miss Warren has found herself other interests on her Connecticut weekends."

His sarcasm made Nicola frown. "Don't be ridiculous," she snapped. "Why should you want to share a sublet with me?"

"Because I need a secretary . . . and a housekeeper . . ."

"And a driver . . ." Nicola put in, beginning to see the light.

"That, too," he added grudgingly. "It's going to be the devil to get around for a couple of weeks. Any more questions?"

"Just one. Why don't you come on home . . . you could relax here and let William take care of you."

"The fact that I've sprained an ankle doesn't mean that I plan to take up permanent residence in a rocking chair. And if I have to sit twiddling my thumbs for a couple of weeks, I prefer to do it where there's sunshine and a swimming pool. I even thought *you* might enjoy it."

That comment made Nicola's jaw drop. Never before in her association with Alex Laird had he evinced the slightest interest in her likes or dislikes. She swallowed and finally managed to say, "Of course, it would be very nice . . ."

"That sounds better. See if you can get a plane tomorrow. The San Diego airport's practically in the middle of town, so you won't have any trouble taking a cab to the Coronado Towers. Juliette said the apartment number is 616."

"You mean, Juliette's going to be there, too?"

"Not in *my* apartment . . ." he hedged.

"Nearby?"

He brushed that aside. "I understand her family has one in the building. You'd better bring the prop list for that American Girl sportswear account. We might be able to get some work done around the apartment if the weather's decent."

"What about a model? Or were you thinking of Juliette for that, too?"

"She did mention it, but I didn't promise anything. That decision can be made after you get there. I could use your help."

His last comment would have aroused more of Nicola's sympathy if she'd thought for a minute that it was really true. If ever a man didn't require assistance in his dealings with the opposite sex, it was Alex Laird.

When Nicola thought about it, she realized that he was being more evasive than usual—which made her suspect that Juliette had over-

played her hand in Mexico City. Even so, Alex
wasn't in full retreat; he had simply chosen a
delaying action. Only, this time, his secretary
would be on the premises to avoid any further
emotional entanglements.

"When I hired you, I wasn't aware that a
long-distance phone call sent you into a trance
every other sentence."

Alex's biting remark brought Nicola erect.
"I'm sorry," she mumbled. "I guess I don't
make much sense so early in the morning."

"I'll remember that in the future," he taunt-
ed. "Do you want me to spell it out again in
words of one syllable?"

"Of course not. Do I have to leave tomorrow?"

"I'd prefer it. Why? Does it interfere with
your social life?"

"As a matter of fact, it does. I had a dinner
date."

"Then break it. He'll still be there when you
get back. A little reluctance helps." The stony
silence that followed his remark made him finally ask, "Are you still there?"

"I was checking my bank balance," she informed him politely, "and I find that I can't afford to quit or get fired this week."

There was another pause while he digested
that. When he spoke again, his tone was carefully polite. "Then I gather that I'll have the
pleasure of your company' in the next day or
so."

"Yes, Mr. Laird." There was no faulting her response now. "Shall I bring the more urgent queries with me as well as the prop list for the sportswear pictures?"

"Might as well." There was a pause, and Nicola heard him speak to someone in the background before he came back on the wire. "Juliette's got a cab waiting downstairs . . . I'll have to go. Any more questions?"

Just one, Nicola wanted to say. Why am I such an utter fool as to still be hanging around? Aloud she said tonelessly, "No, there's nothing more, Mr. Laird. Have a nice flight, and take care of your ankle."

"Don't worry . . . Juliette's playing the heavy nursemaid. See you in San Diego, Nicola."

She slammed her receiver down and glared at it for a minute, while she thought about Juliette fluttering over Alex Laird. It was a pity the model couldn't have donned a nurse's uniform to complete the "angel-of-mercy" picture. The prospect of that was so ludicrous that Nicola had to laugh at herself as she reached for the intercom button. When William answered, she spoke in her usual cheerful tones. "Mr. Laird asked me to meet him in San Diego tomorrow. Do you want me to take anything special along?"

"If you could manage another bag"—William sounded apologetic—"Mr. Alex did ask for some warm-weather clothing when I talked to him."

"Then you knew about this?"

"He just announced that he'd sprained his ankle . . . he didn't mention any details."

Nicola reported all she'd heard. "Apparently Mr. Laird has just arranged to sublet a condominium in San Diego. I suppose there's some staff to help run it, because other than keeping abreast of urgent business, the doctors have ordered complete rest for him."

"That's the very best thing. I'll call our family doctor and find out who Mr. Alex should consult in San Diego. You can see to that once you get there." William had lived with the Lairds long enough to give orders in the same style. "And, of course, Mr. Alex would like his fishing rod. . . ."

"His what?"

"Mr. Alex mentioned that he wanted to try some sport-fishing as long as he was close to Baja California."

Nicola could visualize her arrival on the West Coast laden with her employer's luggage and rod cases. "San Diego's close to the Coast Range, too. Are you sure he doesn't want some mountaineering gear?"

William ignored her sarcasm. "I shouldn't think so. Not with an injured ankle. If he goes sport-fishing, I trust you'll hire a boat that's comfortably outfitted."

Nicola closed her eyes, wondering how a morning that had started out in such promising fashion could have deteriorated so quickly.

"Well, if I can't find one, I'm sure that Miss Denver will take care of things."

"Miss Denver?" William's bland manner cracked slightly.

"Juliette Denver . . . the model who's with Mr. Laird in Mexico City. San Diego is her hometown, so she's arranging for the apartment."

"Mr. Laird told me that he was staying in a condominium with you." William's tone was starched and emphatic.

"I think he will be, but—"

"Then I can't see where this Miss—Denver, was it?—is of the slightest importance."

His autocratic pronouncement made Nicola want to fly up the front stairs and hug his spare elderly frame. "Juliette Denver is a very choice brunette," she said eventually, feeling she should make things clear. "Mr. Laird mentioned how efficiently she was taking care of things."

"If I were you, Miss Nicola . . . I'd call about your plane reservation first thing," William said in a voice of quiet determination. "Obviously there's no time to lose." Then he went on in bracing tones, "I'm sure everything will turn out for the best. Mr. Alex needs a vacation, and you're sure to enjoy the sunshine out there. I'm told that San Diego's climate is almost perfect the year round."

Nicola had occasion to remember his final comment when she emerged from the San

Diego airport late the next evening. There had been balmy Indian-summer weather when her plane left New York, but she'd landed five hours later in the midst of a full-blown southern California thunderstorm. Rain had lashed the passengers as they deplaned down a flight of uncovered steel stairs, and it was still pelting down as Nicola waited at the curb in front of the terminal for a taxi. She stood shivering under a narrow canopy, trying to brush the raindrops from the shoulders of her gabardine suit. It was an outfit that had been recommended for California sunshine by a salesgirl who had never strayed from the steam heat of Manhattan. Nicola thought about her and a raincoat which was still hanging in her office closet. She muttered a few choice phrases that would have made William raise his eyebrows if he'd been within hearing range rather than in a snug townhouse three thousand miles away. She wrapped her arms around her chest to generate more heat and managed to wince only slightly when a case of Alex's fishing rods slithered off the pile of luggage by her feet and landed on her instep. It was fortunate that just then a cab drew up in front of her and she was able to duck inside it. Even when it turned out that the cases of fishing rods could only ride in her lap, she was too tired to argue.

The ride to Coronado was long enough for the cabdriver to tell Nicola that the rain was "most unusual" and a real blessing. She politely refrained from saying that New Yorkers described downpours with many adjectives but "blessing" was seldom applied. Instead she managed to admire the long, graceful bridge they were crossing. It curved high above San Diego Bay to make Coronado and the rest of the peninsula more accessible to the downtown area. "Not as colorful as our old ferries, but lots faster," the driver told her.

As another streak of lightning illuminated the black sky, and the thunder rumbled around them, Nicola shivered in her damp suit and tried to think of something cheerful. At least she wouldn't have to face Alex's critical gaze in her wrinkled state. Just before leaving Manhattan, William had reported that their employer was remaining an extra day in Los Angeles because the San Diego apartment was still being readied for occupancy. Nicola was to stay at the famous old Del Coronado Hotel until he arrived the next day.

The cabdriver drew up under the cone-shaped entrance and obligingly helped transfer the luggage and Alex's fishing rods into the hands of a gray-haired bellman. Thunder was still sounding overhead as Nicola registered and was directed past a floodlit patio into a ground-floor room whose old-fashioned windows faced the ocean. By then she was too sleepy to do more than hang up her clothes in an oversized closet and spread an extra blanket on her bed before she tumbled into it. She was still thinking about leaving a wake-up call with the operator when she snuggled into the pillow and promptly went to sleep.

2

Nicola's slumbers were deep but not entirely undisturbed. Once, the noise of a landing jet aircraft was loud enough to bring her bolt upright and blinking. She soon remembered where she was and that she'd been told about the nearby naval air station north of the hotel. By then, the jet had passed safely overhead, and Nicola plopped down on her bed again, relieved to find that the plane's landing gear hadn't taken off the hotel roof as it had threatened. The rain beating on her windows showed the storm still raged outside, but it was warm and comfortable under the covers, and she was smiling as she again drifted off to sleep.

Even the noise of the telephone on the bedside table at her elbow didn't disturb her unduly when it sounded some hours later. Her midnight plan to leave a wake-up call merely crystallized into reality, and she picked up the receiver expecting to hear the polite tones of an operator saying, "Good morning . . . it's now eight o'clock and our San Diego weather is sunny and warm."

What she was not expecting was a familiar male voice growling, "Nicola? Are you going to sleep all day? Good God—it's almost noon."

"Alex!" Nicola sat upright so fast that she collided with the shade on the bed lamp and found herself steadying the dented parchment with one hand while she struggled to grasp the receiver with the other. "Mr. Laird, I didn't know you were here. That is—where are you?"

"You must be more tired than I thought. What do you mean—'where are you?'"

"I don't see anything wrong in a simple question." Nicola was wishing she could start over again. "William said you were in Los Angeles."

"I was . . . yesterday morning. Today I'm in San Diego. Out in the lobby of your hotel, in case you're interested. I came over three hours ago to take you to breakfast, and have been cooling my heels ever since. If you can finally get vertical, I'll now take you to lunch."

Nicola was having a hard time sorting things out. "You mean you've been waiting in the lobby all this time?"

"Not exactly. I was at the apartment for a while. Look"—he sounded impatient—"we can discuss it over lunch. Okay? How long will it take you to get ready?"

She tried to think. "Twenty minutes."

"I'll give you twenty-five." There was an undercurrent of amusement in his deep voice.

"You'll find me in the dining room next to a cup of coffee."

"All right, thanks." Nicola managed to sound reasonably calm in the circumstances. There was a difference being invited to lunch with her employer in an elegant hotel dining room rather than sharing coffee over a desktop in Manhattan.

"Are you still there, or have you gone back to sleep again?"

She came back to the present in a hurry. "I'm still here."

"You'd better be. I warn you . . . if you're five minutes late, I'll come pounding on your door." Nicola's pulse rate had just started to accelerate when his next remark sent it back to normal. "I'm starving . . . I haven't had anything to eat since coffee and doughnuts at six this morning."

"Then I'll hang up," she responded crisply. "I'd hate to be responsible for a case of malnutrition in addition to your other ailments." She dropped the receiver back in its cradle before he could reply, and swung her legs out of bed, catching up her robe on the way to the shower.

Afterward, she took time to put on a blue suede jumper dress with a tie blouse in a stained-glass print and simply brushed her shoulder-length hair back from her face without trying for the more severe style she usually affected at work.

A minute or so later, she was hurrying across

the patio on the way to the hotel dining room. The sun was trying hard to penetrate the cloud cover, but moisture was still clinging to the palms and oleanders surrounding the colorful inner square. Even so, the air was warm enough to make Nicola's cardigan an unnecessary accessory and she felt suddenly like a tourist carrying an umbrella across the Sahara. By the time she reached the dining-room archway, she had managed to stuff the sweater into her outsized shoulder bag.

As the maitre d' hurried toward her, Nicola was admiring the room's paneled walls and wooden ceiling, which had been carefully preserved from the hotel's turn-of-the-century beginnings. Then she was being led toward a window table at the far end of the big room, where Alex Laird was getting to his feet.

Nicola gave him a tremulous smile as she approached, wondering why the familiar sight of his tall body made her feel breathless and completely uncoordinated. It wasn't that he was any Greek idol; his profile was thoroughly masculine, with a chin that jutted more stubbornly than most, and gray eyes that had been known to wither troublesome account executives in their tracks. The wave in his dark hair was not encouraged, and exercise plus a hard work schedule kept his rangy frame without a spare ounce of flesh. That morning he wore light-weight slacks and a green blazer jacket with careless ease.

Only the new lines around his mouth made Nicola realize that his ankle must be more painful than he was letting on, and she hurriedly let the maitre d' pull out her chair before her employer had to struggle with it. She flashed a smile of thanks over her shoulder and waited until the man had gone on his way before she said, "Please sit down, Mr. Laird—I'm sure you shouldn't be using your ankle so much. Have you seen a doctor here in town?"

Her employer's stern mouth crooked slightly at the corner. "Nicola—you've been around William too long. You're beginning to sound just like him. Whatever happened to 'Good morning' and 'It's nice to see you'?"

She flushed painfully. "I'm sorry, Mr. Laird. I didn't think—"

"Wait a minute," he interrupted. "I object to being called Mr. Laird when we're three thousand miles away from the office. And don't start arguing about it," he said when she would have cut in, "because this time I mean to win. You've called me Alex before this, and nothing catastrophic has happened, so you can abandon those Victorian business ideas. Incidentally, there's a waitress at the next table . . . want some coffee while you're deciding what to eat?"

"Yes, please, Mr. Laird," Nicola said dazedly, wondering what had happened to the man across the table from her in the week he'd been away.

"You're not paying attention . . ."

His quiet comment cut into her reverie, and she smiled ruefully. "I'm sorry . . . Alex. But William won't approve, you know."

"You might be surprised." He gestured to the waitress and waited until she'd poured coffee and taken their order before he directed his gaze to Nicola again. "Did you have a good flight?"

"Fine, thanks." She took a sip of coffee and sat back with a happy sigh. "This is a gorgeous place. I don't even mind if it rains all the time while we're here. Is the apartment nearby?"

"Just a block and a half away. It belongs to Juliette's aunt, who's spending a year abroad." He seemed to be choosing his next words carefully. "When I checked in there this morning, I found that a few things aren't quite as I anticipated."

Nicola's eyebrows rose. "Good or bad?"

Alex shifted uncomfortably. "Just . . . different. For one thing, there's a cook-house-keeper named Maria who was supposed to be living with us. She informed me that her daughter's having a baby and she wants time off to be with her. That's not all bad," he went on before Nicola could comment. "Maria never stops talking . . . whether you can understand her or not. Apparently she came over from Naples just last year. At least, that's what I think she said. And she goes with the apartment, so there's no use trying to bring somebody else in." He watched a smile play over

Nicola's face and started to relax. He should have known that she wouldn't be upset. "You don't mind, then?"

"I don't see why I should. Not if you don't expect gourmet dinners every night that she's away. My talents run more to short orders and calling the local pizza parlor."

He made a careless gesture. "I wasn't concerned about that at all. I thought you might be worried about your reputation if Maria can't get back to the apartment every night to chaperon us. Of course, you don't know anybody out here, which helps. . . ."

"Why should that matter? I'm twenty-four years old—"

"For lord's sake, don't take my head off." Alex frowned back at her. "I don't know what age has to do with it. I thought women cared about those things."

Nicola wanted to point out a long list of women that he'd taken out who hadn't cared in the least about such things. His words had made her feel like an endangered species of womanhood, and a not very appealing one, at that. "I'm sure that everything will be perfectly all right. After all, it's only for two weeks . . . not the rest of our lives," she commented stiffly.

Alex shot her a suspicious glance before he murmured something conventional in an undertone that didn't carry across the damask between them.

Fortunately, their eggs Benedict arrived then, and the subject was dropped by mutual consent while they applied themselves to more important matters.

Afterward, when Alex had paid the bill and gotten to his feet, Nicola slowed her steps to his as they made their way out of the dining room. "You didn't answer my question about the doctor," she reminded him. "Have you seen one since you've been here?"

"There hasn't been time. I told you . . . I just got in this morning."

"Well, in Los Angeles, then. When you were with Juliette."

He pulled up by the bell captain's desk at the edge of the lobby. "I wasn't 'with Juliette' in Los Angeles for any longer than it takes to change planes," he said curtly. "I'd arranged an overnight fishing trip to the Coronado Islands, and Juliette had plans of her own in Pasadena. I told her you'd call when we're ready to start shooting that sportswear sequence."

Nicola was aghast. "You mean, you've already been on a fishing trip with that ankle?"

"I could hardly leave it behind." He turned to beckon to a gray-haired bellman, and then spared her an aloof glance. "Is your stuff ready in the room?" When she nodded, he began making arrangements with the man to have it transferred to the condominium on the beach.

Nicola moved over to the cashier's window to check out and was informed that her account had already been settled by Mr. Laird earlier in the morning.

"I would have told you," came his voice behind her when she started to turn away, "that is, if you'd waited around."

"I'm used to paying my own hotel bills. . . ."

"Then this will be a new experience for you," he cut in, leading her toward the hotel's entrance. "Relax and enjoy it." He winced suddenly as he put his weight on his left foot when they started down the steps.

"Here . . . lean on me." Nicola was gazing at him with a worried expression. "You shouldn't be moving around so much."

"I'll vegetate for a while when we get back to the apartment. It won't be much fun for you."

"It might be a new experience," she quoted with a mischievous look, and reached for the car key in his hand. "Are you parked nearby?"

"Just over there." He indicated a white station wagon on the curve of the drive. "I take it you're driving?"

"Absolutely. I have to do something to earn my salary."

It was less than five minutes later that she was parking again, this time in a reserved space by a tall condominium which overlooked the Pacific on one side and San Diego's scenic Glorietta Bay on the other. The building facade was an attractive combination of textured stone and floor-to-ceiling windows that allowed residents to take advantage of the magnificent views. Each apartment included a lanai, as well, which provided a festive note, with sun furniture and containers of bright flowers in terra-cotta containers at the railings.

"You'd never know it was October, would you?" Nicola asked after she'd gotten out of the car and stood for a moment taking in the opulent surroundings. "I can't think why Juliette's aunt would want to forsake all this for a trip abroad."

"Especially the Costa del Sol, where the hotels never have enough heat in the winter," Alex declared. "I'm glad she did, though. The prospect of being lazy here for a week or so sounds better all the time. I understand there's a nice pool on the ocean side of the building," he went on casually, gesturing her toward the apartment entrance. "Let's take a look at it. I think there's a door at the back of the lobby."

They made their way through a lush secluded patio that showed evidence of expensive landscape gardening with its thick plantings of tropical shrubs and palms.

The condominium lobby beyond was almost a solarium, with big windows and a native stone floor. There was a continuation of the outside plantings—only this time the philodendrons and hibiscus were in planters rather than well-tended beds. Two elevators occupied the far wall of the lobby and the only other sign of habitation was a recessed office area almost hidden by a bank of plants at the rear. Evidently the tenants of the tower didn't want commercialism to seep into their world, Nicola thought with some amusement. Since the two mahogany desks in the office cubicle were deserted at that moment, privacy was easy to achieve.

"I understand there's a doorman here at night," Alex said, as he saw her frankly curious gaze. "The rest of the security people hide in the shrubbery. I don't mean literally," he added with a grin as he saw her turn to give an incredulous look behind them. "They just try to stay out of sight. Juliette said something about a resident manager, but he hasn't shown. . . ."

Nicola caught sight of a tall young man coming toward them from a door marked "Pool Area" at the end of the hallway, and murmured, "Not until now. I think you're about to have the pleasure."

There wasn't time for Alex to do more than follow her glance before a redheaded man in his late twenties who was clad in an expensive sport coat and slacks came up to them and stuck out his hand. "Mr. Laird? Juliette said you'd be coming along this morning. I'm sorry to have missed you earlier." He turned to Nicola with scarcely a pause. "I'm Kevin Graham, the manager here, and you must be Nicola. Juliette's told me about you, too. Welcome to San Diego."

Nicola couldn't help smiling at Kevin Graham's enthusiastic manner as she found her

hand being shaken firmly, as well. "Thank you.
I'm sure that I'm going to like it here," she replied.

Alex's response showed that he wasn't so
impressed. "Is there anything Juliette didn't
tell you?" he inquired of the manager politely.

"Not very much." Kevin's grin stayed firmly
in place. "Our tenants require a pretty complete dossier on any newcomers, and once
Juliette explained about you—well, we're delighted that you've decided to stay. And Miss
Warren, as well." He bent toward Alex in a
confidential manner. "Don't blame Juliette for
the mix-up about Maria—these things happen.
When I learned a little while ago that the
woman was going to desert you until her
daughter's baby arrives, I called Juliette first
thing to ask what she wanted to do."

Nicola's feeling of well-being vanished and
she saw a frown crease Alex's forehead. "Why
was it necessary to bother Miss Denver about
something like that?" she asked in the awkward
silence.

The manager discarded his professional
facade; he was merely a troubled young man as
he stared back at her. "I had to," he said.
"Juliette's in charge of her aunt's property
while she's away, so the building management
had no legal alternative. Besides, I've known
Miss Denver for years, and I felt she could
come up with a solution for Mr. Laird if anyone could."

"Thanks," Alex commented dryly.

Kevin Graham hurried on as if he'd barely heard him. "Juliette said that the main reason you'd needed Maria was simply to serve as a chaperon for the two of you."

"There was a small matter of cooking and cleaning the apartment," Alex put in.

Kevin waved that aside. "We can find someone for those duties, but Juliette didn't know of anyone else to live in the apartment with you—on such short notice. She said there was really only one solution."

Alex held up a palm. "Let me guess. Juliette's going to come down and stay with us. Am I right?"

The manager beamed. "That's it exactly. She'll catch an afternoon flight and be with you this evening." He bestowed a kindly glance on Nicola. "She said to tell you not to bother cooking an elaborate dinner—anything will do."

"I see." The tone of Nicola's voice showed that she saw only too well.

"No, you don't," Alex cut in so forcibly that they both gave a start of surprise. "All this is completely unnecessary . . . there's no reason whatsoever for Juliette to change her plans."

"But with Maria taking time off . . ." Kevin began.

"Frankly, I couldn't care less." Alex groped for Nicola's hand and enclosed it firmly in his. "Juliette doesn't realize that Nicola is more than just my secretary"—his grip tightened on the slim fingers under his—"she also happens to be my wife . . . and we're long past the stage of needing a live-in chaperon. Isn't that right, darling?" He bent over Nicola, outwardly the solicitous husband, but in actuality bestowing a fierce look that dared her to contradict him.

Nicola was so astounded that she wouldn't have questioned the presence of her guardian angel if he'd suddenly appeared at her side. In fact, she would have welcomed any volunteer to help care for her employer, who apparently had gone clean off his rocker. It must be some medication they'd given him for his ankle, she thought frantically, and wondered how best to humor him.

"Wake up, woman!" Alex gave her a shake before turning back to Kevin. "That's what jet lag does to a person. I think I'll have to put my wife back to bed."

"I'm terribly sorry . . . I didn't realize . . ." Kevin Graham's cheeks took on the fiery shade of his hair as he stumbled through the apology. "Naturally, you won't want . . ."

"Houseguests?" Alex's grin was thoroughly masculine. "Hardly. We haven't been married *that* long." He tucked Nicola's limp hand under his elbow in a proprietary manner. "If you'll get in touch with Juliette, I'd appreciate it," he went on to the manager. "It would be foolish for her to make an unnecessary trip down here."

"I'll try." The other man was pathetically eager to please. "Will you be in the building for the next hour or so?"

Nicola opened her lips to reply, but Alex cut her off smoothly again. " 'Fraid not. We just stopped by to get an extra key to the apartment for my wife, but I'm sure you can arrange that without our hanging around. We have an appointment downtown." He managed to glance at his watch even as he tugged Nicola toward the big glass doors. "Nice to have met you, Graham . . . you'll have to come up and have a drink with us once we get settled in." He shoved Nicola through the doors and out into the patio before either she or Kevin Graham could reply.

Alex appeared to ignore the pain of his ankle, keeping an iron grip on her arm until they were beside the car. "Give me the keys," he commanded her. Then he added, "Don't get any ideas about making a bolt for it. I haven't lost my mind. . . ."

"You're sure? I thought for a minute you needed a psychiatrist instead of an orthopedist."

Alex unlocked the car door and motioned her to the driver's seat. "If I had to live two weeks with Juliette underfoot, I'd need to hire a psychiatrist round the clock. Let's get out of here. There's a drive-in about two blocks down this main street. We can have a cup of coffee and figure out what to do."

Nicola switched on the ignition and followed his directions. "Frankly, I think we're going to need a full-blown miracle at this point." She sneaked a look at him after she turned into the arterial. "I didn't know you were the impulsive type. You never have been before."

"How do you know?" The curtness in his voice showed that he was fast reverting to normal. "You sound like some kind of therapist."

"There's no need to snarl at me because you lost your head. Anyone would think Juliette had the whammy on you," Nicola told him, forgetting that proper secretaries don't argue with their employers. Not if they expect to collect their old-age benefits.

Alex's stern expression showed he hadn't overlooked that point, even if she had. "Park in there," he said austerely, indicating a drive-in in the middle of the block. "We'll discuss this after we've ordered."

Nicola couldn't very well say she was already awash with coffee, that she'd prefer an aspirin instead for the headache that she was sure he was going to give her. Instead she sat meekly behind the wheel until the waitress had delivered their coffee. She even took a sip of it, keeping her gaze fixed on the windshield while she said to Alex, "Obviously I'd better go back to New York as soon as possible. You can make some sort of explanation to Juliette. Tell her I'm allergic to smog or salt air or something."

Alex gave a snort of disgust and rested his coffee mug on the dashboard. "I'll do nothing of the sort, and you're certainly not going back to New York. I haven't changed my mind about wanting you here."

"But that was before all this happened!"

"Oh, for God's sake, Nicola . . . don't belabor the obvious." He took a deep breath and went on. "Sorry, I didn't mean to shout at you. Be a good girl and listen to what I have to say, will you?"

"I'm listening."

He took a sip of coffee before going on. "There's only one way to carry through on this . . . we'll have to get married."

"I beg your pardon," Nicola said finally over the roaring in her ears. "Would you repeat that?"

"I just said," Alex announced with terrible patience, "that we'll have to get married."

"That's what I thought. Are you sure you didn't bruise your head in Mexico City?"

"I know somebody else who'll be bruised in a minute," he warned. "Look, I'll admit that I should have consulted you before I said anything to that fellow."

"I should hope so. . . ."

"But that's beside the point now," he continued without a pause. "Actually, there's a simple solution to this right across the border. A Mexican marriage takes care of all our problems while we're here. We can have it dissolved when we get back to New York—it's no problem at all for a good lawyer. I'm surprised I didn't think of it before."

Nicola rubbed her forehead with fingers that trembled. After the months she had spent working with Alex Laird, she'd thought there was nothing that he could do to surprise her. She'd also thought that "marriage" was not an acceptable word in his bachelor's vocabulary. Yet, here he was, talking about taking the fatal step as calmly as he'd discuss the stock-market report. She replaced her cup on the drive-in tray. "I think," she said, "that I need something stronger than coffee."

"Later." A strange smile flickered over his face. "You take a lot of convincing."

"Well, hearing you propose marriage—even for a weekend—makes about as much sense as Casanova signing up for holy orders."

The smile disappeared. "Thanks very much," he said stiffly. "It's nice to know what you think."

"I didn't mean that like it sounds. It's just that I thought you enjoyed your freedom."

"If you'd listen to what I'm saying, you'd understand," he replied with some asperity. "I said that a Mexican marriage was the best solution to our problem . . . not the ideal one."

His cold appraisal made any possible romantic hopes that Nicola might have cherished immediately wither on the vine. She tried to keep her voice as dispassionate as his. "It seems like a great furore over very little. All you have to do is tell Juliette the truth and ask her to keep quiet."

"Do you seriously think that would have any effect? Even if we denied the whole thing now, she'd spread the word around Manhattan and put her own embellishments on every juicy tidbit. We'd both look like fools."

Nicola thought for a minute of his business acquaintances who would relish the thought of such scandal, and nodded reluctantly. "I suppose you're right." Then, trying to salvage her feminine pride, she asked, "You're sure that it's easy to dissolve a Mexican marriage?"

Alex was quick to recognize her weakening. "Of course. Besides, there's a damned good reason why I can't pull up stakes and leave here right now." He saw her puzzled frown and said, "I can explain it on the way to Tijuana."

"You mean . . . we should drive down there right now?"

"Well, there's no point in waiting." He handed her his empty coffee mug and rummaged in his coat pocket. "I've some notes on Mexican marriage requirements here someplace. . . ."

Nicola's eyes narrowed. "That's very convenient."

"You needn't look so suspicious. A fellow on the fishing boat was telling me that he takes people down to Baja all the time. Couples who want to combine fishing trips and honeymoons," he explained, pulling out a printed brochure.

"Fishing trips and honeymoons . . ." she muttered dazedly.

"Uh-huh." Alex wasn't paying particular attention. "Can't say that I think much of the copywriting on this."

She looked over his shoulder and read aloud. " 'The best of all sports' . . . what do they mean by that?"

"Who knows?" Alex turned to the back cover of the booklet. "Here we are. They recommend a tourist card . . . but I think we could do without that in Tijuana. How about your birth certificate?"

"Would a passport do?" Nicola reached for her purse. "I've gotten used to carrying mine when I travel with you. This isn't the first time that our itinerary's been changed."

"It wasn't my fault that the weather was rotten in Trinidad last spring. Besides, the switch to Barbados for those background shots worked out very well. The client was sorry he didn't think of it first." Alex plucked her passport out of her hand and opened it. "This passport picture makes you look like the lead character in a neighborhood wake."

Nicola snatched her passport back. "I'll hire a better photographer next time."

"You mean I took that? Let me have another look."

"Never mind." She put the passport in her purse. "What else do the Mexicans require?"

He turned back to the brochure. "A marriage license and a medical certificate. We can take care of that easily enough. Let's get started."

"But where are we going?" Nicola's question was almost a wail.

"Back to the main street here and turn left. This highway intersects with the freeway south and takes you straight to the border." Alex leaned across her to pay the bill and signal for the drive-in waitress to remove their tray. "I wish that this damned ankle of mine didn't make driving so difficult," he muttered irritably.

"I don't care about that . . . so long as you'll navigate," Nicola said, starting the car. "Do you know where we go in Tijuana? I read that there are two hundred thousand people living there now. We can't cruise up and down the street looking for a justice of the peace."

"Certainly not." Alex settled back. "I'll direct you to the courthouse once we get across the border. That's where we find the *Juez del Registro Público* who performs the ceremony after we take care of the technicalities."

"Was all that information in your booklet?"

"Most of it. Right along with the kind of tackle to bring." He caught her sideways glance. "For the fishing trip afterward."

"That," she told him as she accelerated down the busy highway, "was what I hoped you meant."

They drove past the condominium on the way south, and Nicola remembered how uncluttered her life had been just an hour before, when she'd first seen the apartment building which was even now disappearing in the rear-vision mirror. Alex might have been thinking the same thing, because he did nothing to break the silence between them as the car went on past some naval installations on the beach to their right and a cluster of new housing units facing the bay on their left.

It was Nicola who finally took her glance from the traffic long enough to say, "You promised to tell me why we have to stay around and face the music." An amused note crept into her voice. "You didn't step on somebody's toes in Mexico City, did you? Things were calm enough in Manhattan before you left, so something must have happened down there."

"As a matter of fact, you're not far wrong." Alex gave Nicola's profile a considering glance. "It was something I stumbled onto when I was getting permission to use Chapultepec Castle as a location for the fashion photographs. It turned out that the Mexican official in charge of national museums and antiquities was Marco Alvarez—a fellow I knew in college."

He fell silent as Nicola accelerated to the faster lane of the highway, which was merging with the main freeway, until she sent him a prompting glance. By then, she had discovered that it was better to concentrate on his story than dwell on what was going to happen once they reached Tijuana.

If Alex suspected her reasons, he didn't give any indication. His voice was expressionless as he continued with his story. "Marco invited me out to his home in honor of old times while I was there, and he seemed especially interested when I told him that I was going to vacation in San Diego while I was waiting for my ankle to heal."

"You've lost me. What does San Diego have to do with Mexico City?"

"I wanted to know the same thing. That was when he asked me how much I knew about the history of Chapultepec." Alex shifted on the seat so that he could watch Nicola's calm profile. "You've seen the castle, haven't you? When you vacationed down there last year?"

She nodded slowly, trying to remember. "I went through it the first day. There were scads of tourists all over the place. Maximilian and Carlota lived there for a short time."

"Until their reign was overthrown and Maximilian was finally killed," Alex said. "I imagine he often wandered through Chapultepec wishing he was back in his castle at Miramare in Italy. A beautiful spot near Trieste," he added in explanation. "Unfortunately, neither Maximilian nor Carlota ever returned to it."

There was a moment of silence while both of them thought of that imposing but unhappy castle on the hill in Mexico City where the ill-fated monarchs had lived until political fortunes changed.

Then Alex shook his head slightly as if to clear it and said, "The Mexican government has been repairing the castle foundations in the south wing this past year and demolished an old wall in the course of their restoration. One day they came upon a cache of jewelry and silver that had belonged to the Empress. Naturally, they were overjoyed, because they thought the treasures had been looted at the time of the monarchy's downfall. Marco told me that the next day they found a small leather trunk in an unauthorized excavation just beyond the wall."

"What did they find in the trunk? More jewelry, or the family silver?" Nicola asked excitedly.

"Neither one. Just an empty trunk. Somebody had beaten them to it. That day two of the workmen didn't appear on the job, so it wasn't hard to figure out what happened. When the authorities went to their homes, they found the body of one of them. The other man had simply disappeared. . . ."

"Taking all the goodies with him," Nicola finished. "Couldn't they find him—at least they knew who it was?"

"Mexico is a big country and still undeveloped in the major parts. Marco told me that their authorities sent out feelers to all the major cities. After that, they just had to sit back and wait."

"But where does San Diego come into it?"

"About a month ago, the man they wanted was reported to have been seen talking business with an American in Puerto Vallarta. At the time, the Mexican was working with the charter fishing crews there, but before the police could make an arrest, he had disappeared again. They suspect that he was murdered, but they haven't found a body."

"So the Mexican officials are concentrating on the West Coast fishing fleets and hoping to turn up some evidence?"

"Something like that. They think the treasure will eventually be sold in this country. Marco knew that I planned to do some sportfishing and thought I might hear something around the charter crews. Especially if I went down to Baja for a weekend and anchored at Ensenada. He claims that the natives can tell if a Mexican policeman is within five miles. On the other hand, an American fisherman could hear whether anybody was showing unusual signs of prosperity around the docks or drinking too much at the cantina."

"He might also get his throat cut if he asked too many questions," Nicola pointed out.

"Naturally, he'd have to be discreet. But everybody knows that fishermen and commercial photographers are eccentric to start with. When they're Americans to boot—they have an open field."

"Especially if the photographer travels with his secretary."

"His wife," Alex corrected swiftly. "Everything aboveboard and beyond suspicion."

"His wife, then," she managed to say.

"Except that you're not going along on any Mexican fishing trips. It won't matter on the stuff around San Diego," he added magnanimously.

"Well, I like that," she protested, half-turning to confront him. There was a honk from the car beside them when her attention wandered.

"Watch where you're going!" Alex sounded like a husband already as he watched her correct her steering.

"You don't have to behave as if I needed a learner's permit," she told him when the station wagon was back where it belonged.

"You do that again, my girl, and we'll be in the Tijuana hospital for more than a quick blood test," he warned.

Nicola ignored him, wondering whether she should make an issue out of the fishing trips. She had every intention of accompanying him, whether he liked it or not, but there was no point in telling him so at this juncture. She chose a convenient change of subject instead. "It looks like we're approaching the border. Either that or there's an almighty traffic jam ahead of us."

"It's the border, all right. The Mexican customs men usually just wave the tourists through."

She braked carefully to avoid any more critical comments on her driving. "You're sure that this is the best thing for us to do? I could still make a U-turn."

"On a six-lane freeway?" He shuddered. "No way."

"Well, I could tell the immigration people that I just wanted to turn around," she said, not knowing why she felt like a bullfighter facing a monumental "moment of truth."

"Don't be an idiot. Pull up in that line over there behind the Volkswagen."

She did as he suggested but gritted her teeth and said, "For two cents, Alex Laird, I'd head back—"

He interrupted her calmly. "Try to look happy, will you? Otherwise, they'll think we're already married."

Nicola braked with a snap that almost threw him against the windshield. "I'm sorry about that," she said when he turned toward her with a thunderous expression.

"I'll bet." Alex resisted an urge to throttle her in front of the entire border forces of two countries. "Just you wait," he gritted out, before nodding to the inspector who appeared beside the car.

The Mexican official scarcely bothered to look at them. "What is the purpose of your visit to Mexico?" he droned.

"We want to get married," Alex said in a loud, defiant tone.

There was a snort from Nicola's side of the car.

"Bueno!" The official beamed at them, coming to life. "There's nothing so nice as meeting a betrothed couple. Believe me, I envy you in this time of such great happiness with each other."

3

In the normal run of things, Nicola would have apologized for her bad temper sometime within the next half-hour. Alex, too, was prone to explosive outbursts which seldom lasted more than five minutes before he forgot about them. That afternoon in Tijuana, however, they both found the facade of icy politeness the easiest attitude to maintain: Alex because he soon discovered that getting married in Mexico wasn't as easy as he had professed, and Nicola because she didn't want to reveal that she was as nervous as a half-grown kitten in unfamiliar territory.

Unfortunately, neither had any idea of the other's true thoughts.

Alex kept a determined grip on Nicola's elbow as they waded through Mexican red tape in applying for the license and the medical certificates before finally making their way back to the proper courtroom for the brief ceremony. By then Nicola was only capable of polite monosyllables and looked so pale that it was a wonder she'd passed the medical exam.

When the small, gray-haired Mexican judge finally uttered the final words of the ceremony, he beamed and shook hands vigorously with the dazed couple.

They were out on the steps of the courthouse clutching the precious marriage certificate before Alex realized that he'd over-looked the old American custom of kissing the bride. He shot a guilty look at Nicola's drawn profile and decided against trying to remedy his oversight just then.

Instead he said, "Well, we made it," and started guiding her down the crowded sidewalk toward their parked car. When his brilliant remark met with no response, he tried to do better. "Would you like to look around town a little? Not that there's much to shop for in this section," he added, noting the tourist gimcracks piled in the display windows lining the sidewalk. "There are some decent stores by the jai-alai arena, but that's quite a ways from here. Or we could have something to drink—the local beer's good." As he rattled on, he became aware that he was sounding like a volunteer for the local Chamber of Commerce. Another look at Nicola's quiet figure beside him showed that she wasn't enthusiastic about any of the offers. "Maybe you'd rather go back to the apartment," he said finally. "You look beat."

That brought response of a sort. Color

washed across her cheekbones, and she managed a quick glance at him before staring straight ahead again. "It has been a long day," she agreed. "If you don't mind, I'd like to go on back."

"Of course." Alex felt a twinge of remorse which was new to him and then found himself ushering her protectively past a sidewalk salesman who was insistent that they look over his tray of bracelets and rings. "Not now," Alex told him tersely, and walked on beside Nicola in silence until they reached the station wagon.

She was waiting for him to unlock the car door when he saw a flicker of interest cross her features. He followed her gaze to a nearby window display of ceramic tiles decorated with Spanish inscriptions.

"See something you like?" he asked, being careful to keep his tone impersonal.

"Those tiles." Nicola moved over to the show window and peered through the glass. "They're pretty."

Alex shoved the car keys back in his pocket and followed her. "Can you translate the mottos?"

"Most of them." Nicola was beginning to sound more like her normal self. "There's a favorite of mine. *¡Qué bonito es no hacer nada, y despues de no hacer nada, descansar!*"

" 'How splendid it is to do nothing, and after doing nothing, to rest,' " he translated. "I think we should have that one."

"Just a second." She caught his sleeve when he would have gone in the store. "What does that one in the corner mean?

" '*Meresco más, pero contigo me conformo.*' "

Alex stalled for an instant before saying, "It's nothing you'd like."

"That's possible, but what does it say?"

He translated reluctantly. " 'I deserve better, but I'll go along with you.' "

Nicola's lashes came down to hide her hurt reaction. "You'd better buy that one as a souvenir of the occasion," she said finally. "It's nice and noncommittal—just like everything else today. In case we need reminding."

"Whatever you say," Alex tossed her the car keys. "I'll go in and buy it while you wait in the car," he said. Privately he was kicking himself for translating the damn motto in the first place. Nicola hadn't needed anything else to undermine her self-confidence.

When he got back to the car a few minutes later with his carefully wrapped package, he was happy to see that Nicola had regained her composure.

She started the motor without saying anything more and pulled slowly out into the street behind a crowded Mexican bus which was belching black exhaust fumes. "Didn't you need Mexican money to buy the tile?" She asked him when the traffic had thinned.

Alex laughed. "I don't think some Tijuana shopkeepers have seen a Mexican peso in years." He kept his voice casual. "Feeling better about things?"

"Yes, thanks." She didn't try to dissemble. "For a minute there, everything was a little overwhelming. I wondered what in the dickens I was doing in Tijuana . . ."

"With a strange man for a husband?"

"How did you know?"

"Because for a minute there, I felt the same way about a brand-new wife. What is it about marriage licenses—even ones written in Spanish—that makes the blood rush to your head?" He grinned wryly. "I'm glad that you're taking on familiar outlines again. The same Nicola who's kept my life on an even keel all these months. Only the name has been changed."

"I just kept your business life on an even keel," Nicola pointed out, feeling like one of his filing cabinets.

"Well, now you can broaden your horizons," Alex said comfortably as he sat back and watched the steady lines of cars which were slowing as they approached the U.S. border. On either side of the road, enterprising Mexicans had set up their wares, hoping to nab a customer caught in the traffic jam. There were the usual pictures painted on velvet, a half-dozen ungainly statues of toreros and their red capes, and occasionally some attractive displays of big terra-cotta flowerpots and waist-high strawberry barrels. There was nothing exciting about it, Alex decided. On the other hand, there was nothing to make Nicola look as subdued as she did. He thought about mentioning it, and then decided not to. The fleeting thought that he was already acting more like a husband than a bachelor brought an ironic look to his own face.

The U.S. immigration inspection at the border station was cursory, but afterward they had to park and wait for the officials to make a customs search of their car.

Nicola had no sooner cut the engine and Alex rolled down his window when they were hailed by the driver of the car parked next to theirs.

"Hey, Alex! I thought you were going to spend the day sleeping," said the big barrel-chested man with sun-streaked hair who got out and came over to the station wagon.

Alex started to laugh, and opened his car door to meet him alongside. "No thanks to you! How are you, Pat?" He bent down to window height and introduced him. "Nicola, this is Patrick Towne—he's captain of the charter boat that I was on last night." Then he glanced over his shoulder. "Pat, this is Nicola . . . my wife." The last two words came out after a barely perceptible pause.

"Your wife! I didn't know you were married." Towne's broad shoulders replaced Alex's at the station-wagon window. "How are you, Nicola? Did you rout Alex out of the sack for a shopping trip down here?"

"Something like that," she said, returning his smile.

"That just goes to show what a blonde can do to a man. Worse than a barracuda anytime." He glanced across at Alex. "Are you on your way home?"

"As soon as we pass inspection." Alex jerked his head toward the customs man who was working his way down the line of cars ahead of them. "It shouldn't be long."

Pat Towne nodded. "Guess I'd better get back to my car and dig out some receipts to have ready. I'm happy to have met you, Nicola," he added hastily, bending down to peer in the station wagon again. "You'll be on our next fishing trip, won't you? Along with Alex?"

"We'll see," Alex replied. "I'm going to put her to work for part of the time while we're in San Diego."

"Don't agree to that," Towne advised her. "He's just afraid you might catch a bigger fish. Husbands can't stand it."

"Are you speaking from experience?" Nicola asked, matching his confidential tone.

"Not personally. I'm not married. That's strictly an observer's viewpoint. You'd be surprised what I see on some of the charter cruises. I could tell you stories you wouldn't believe. . . ."

Alex got back in the station wagon again. "That's why I was up half of last night—I was listening to Pat talk rather than going below and getting some sleep."

"Well, if Nicola comes along next time, I'll make sure to send you off to bed nice and early." Towne laughed at Alex's frown, and went on in a more normal tone. "Seriously, Alex—next trip, don't forget to bring along that book on Chapultepec you were telling me about. I'd like to see the photographs you mentioned."

Alex nodded and slammed the car door. "I won't forget."

Towne gave them a friendly wave and turned back to his car just as the customs man came up to the station wagon on the other side.

The border inspection didn't take long and Nicola managed not to show her surprise when Alex told the inspector that there were two tiles in the package rather than just the one she'd thought he was buying.

Once they had been waved on and were part of the traffic on the freeway back to San Diego, Alex put the package on the back seat and looked at his watch. "We should have enough time to change clothes at the apartment and then go out for dinner. I don't know about you, but getting married has given me an appetite. How does some Italian food sound?"

"Wonderful," Nicola said, before making a grimace. "That takes our measure, doesn't it? I understand real newlyweds don't think of food for a week."

"I don't know what kind of books you read," Alex said severely. "At most of the wedding receptions I've attended, the bridegrooms have spent their entire time hovering around the punchbowl and hors d'oeuvres. One groom got so sloshed that his bride had to drive the getaway car."

"I believe the expression is 'going away,' " Nicola said primly.

"So it is. I stand corrected. What is it in our case? Are we 'going away' or 'coming back'?"

"Coming back, I suppose. Oh, for heaven's sake! Who cares?"

"I just wondered." His expression was all innocence. "And if I were you, I'd stow any thoughts you might have about our marriage not being 'real.' If you'll remember, that judge had other ideas."

"In the legal sense, perhaps."

"Naturally. What else do you think I meant?" he said just as coolly. "Remind me to put aside the book on Chapultepec that Pat mentioned," he went on a minute later. "He's a history buff as well as a damned good fisherman."

"I noticed that he had some other talents, as well."

Alex's eyebrows drew together. "What do you mean by that?"

Nicola decided that it wouldn't hurt Alex to learn that her normal powers of observation hadn't ceased to function when she signed the marriage license. "Just that he fancies himself a

ladies' man. With that physique, I'm not surprised. I think it might be fun for me to try
some sport-fishing while we're here."

"I'll arrange for you to sign on one of the beginners' trips. I doubt if Pat would be interested in having to bait your hook."

Alex's annoyed reply proved that Nicola had
finally struck paydirt. Not unnaturally, she was
loath to abandon her winning attack. "I don't
know about that," she said. "From the way he
talked, I thought I had a definite invitation."

"Let's discuss it another time." Alex's expression showed a twinge of pain as he shifted
his sprained ankle to get more comfortable.
"For the next day or so, you'll be busy around
town. I'm going to need some props so I can
start shooting that sportswear layout this week.
There's no reason why we can't use the apartment lanai as a background for a few of the
shots. Juliette suggested it, as a matter of fact."

"Was that why she was leaping down here at
the first sign of trouble? Or was she just report-
ing early for work?" The angry retort escaped
Nicola before she could stifle it.

It was Alex's turn to look smug. "You heard
what the building manager said. Juliette just
wanted to make sure everything went all right.
Probably she felt responsible, since she sublet
the apartment."

"If she'd wanted to play housemother, she
should have arranged to take Maria's place

from the beginning. Except that she can't cook, can she?"

"I don't know. She didn't have to when she went out with me. I probably should have asked if *you* can."

"I'm awfully good at calling room service and thawing frozen dinners," Nicola said sweetly.

"Never mind, I hear there are lots of fine restaurants in San Diego." Alex sounded tired, and he pulled himself erect in the seat as if it had been a long day.

Nicola's conscience nudged her, and she almost confessed that she didn't need a guide-book when she entered a kitchen, but by then Alex had leaned forward and turned on the car radio as if even a depressing news broadcast was preferable to talking to his bride.

When they arrived back at the condominium a little later, they got out of the car without any more conversation. Alex's ankle was obviously annoying him, but the grim set of his jaw didn't encourage comments on his health.

The lobby was empty as they entered it, and soft recorded music from a ceiling speaker in the elevator was the only sound as they were whisked swiftly to the sixth floor. They emerged into a wide hall carpeted in soft gray-green. There were only four entrance doors opening from it, and Alex led the way toward the one at the far end. He was still searching for his key when the elaborately carved door was pulled abruptly open.

Kevin Graham, the young building manager, had his hand on the knob, but he was looking back into the interior of the apartment as he said, "With any luck, there'll be someone here in the next half-hour or so. Don't move anything until then."

Alex cut in sharply. "What in the hell is going on?"

Graham turned so fast that it was almost comical. When he saw both Nicola and Alex standing there, his face became nearly as red as his hair. "Mr. and Mrs. Laird! I didn't know you were back."

"That's obvious." Alex brushed past him into the apartment foyer and motioned for Nicola to follow.

She had just a moment to notice a spacious living room beyond, which was decorated in green with accents of yellow and white, before Kevin started to stammer out an explanation.

"Someone broke in and rifled the apartment," he said. "Apparently they've gone through your things as well. It must have happened sometime after Maria left at noon. Now that you're back, you can let me know if any of your belongings are missing."

"All right. It shouldn't take long." Alex sounded as if he was nearing the end of his patience. "What I don't understand is how you found out. Was this some sort of a routine security check on your part?"

"Of course not, darling." This time the voice

belonged to the tall, striking dark-haired woman emerging from a bedroom hallway. "Don't start shouting at Kevin—he was only doing his job."

Nicola was so surprised that she put out a hand to steady herself in the doorway. Alex was the one who said, "Juliette . . . what in the devil are you doing here?"

"You should know, darling. I came down to help you out when I heard about the difficulties with Maria." The model smoothed her red-striped tunic top, which she wore over white tailored pants, knowing very well that both men were watching her.

Nicola recognized the studied gesture from past performances at the studio in Manhattan. She also noted that Juliette was her usual immaculate self: not a strand of raven shoulder-length hair was disturbed, and the scarlet shade of her lipstick matched her tunic as well as providing a blaze of color against a skin as white as an early narcissus.

Alex didn't bother with an inventory. Instead, he turned to Kevin Graham with such an annoyed expression that the young man took an instinctive step backward.

"I know what you're thinking . . . but I couldn't reach her. She'd already left," the building manager said. "Naturally, I told her what you said as soon as she arrived."

"Naturally." Juliette sounded aggrieved. "And I certainly wouldn't have come if I'd known the whole story. You might have mentioned your marriage when we were in Mexico City, Alex. We had plenty of time together."

That innuendo made Nicola decide that she'd been ignored quite long enough. "Exactly what I told him," she said to the model, reaching over to catch Alex's hand in a fond clasp, "but you know how men are. It's a shame you made such a useless journey . . ." She broke off at a sudden crash from the living room. "What's that?"

"My God, maybe there's somebody still here." Alex started toward the sound. "Graham, you cover the service entrance."

"Wait a minute—both of you." Juliette's sharp order made them pause. "It's not what you think. I went over the apartment inch by inch when I arrived."

"Well, I certainly heard something," Nicola said defensively.

"I'm not arguing about that," Juliette replied in some satisfaction. "It's just that you have another houseguest."

"What are you talking about?" Alex snarled.

Juliette wasn't to be hurried. "Maria left her cat behind. She said in her note that he was too young to take to her daughter's house at a time like this."

Another noise erupted from the room beyond them; this time a dull, heavy thud.

"Probably the candles on the dining-room table," Juliette commented, as no one seemed

Alive with pleasure!
Newport

©Lorillard, U.S.A., 1976

18 mg. "tar", 1.2 mg. nicotine
av. per cigarette, FTC Report Dec. 1976.

Regular: 5 mg. "tar", 0.4 mg. nicotine av. per cigarette, FTC Report Dec. 1976.
Menthol: 5 mg. "tar", 0.4 mg. nicotine av. per cigarette, by FTC Method.

True slashes tar in half!

Only

5 MGS. TAR

And a taste worth smoking.

inclined to move and find out. "He's fond of rolling them on the floor. If you ask me, he should be named Ivan the Terrible."

The sudden clatter that came a moment later showed that Ivan hadn't overlooked the candlesticks in his sweep; evidently they'd followed the candles over the edge.

"Some honeymoon!" Nicola was barely able to hear Alex's bitter complaint. "To think I turned down a nice quiet hospital room in Mexico City for this."

She gave him a bleak look as she started for the dining room. "Keep that hospital telephone number handy. I may take over your reservation."

4

It was fully an hour later before Nicola was able to think about sinking down on the couch in the living room for a rest.

During the interval, she found it was necessary to shut Ivan into the small storage room off the kitchen. Ivan had turned out to be a beguiling tiger kitten with amber eyes, whose unflagging energy would have put nuclear-power plants to shame. He vigorously protested his incarceration until he found he was in virgin territory and systematically started plunging into the cardboard cartons Maria had left on her daybed. Before Nicola closed the door, she noted that the housekeeper apparently wasn't in the habit of staying overnight in the apartment, because the bed was piled deep with storage items. Only the small adjoining bathroom revealed some of the cook's personal possessions on the shelf of the medicine cabinet. Nicola prudently closed that door, too, before Ivan could enlarge his territory.

Once back in the kitchen, she gave the gleaming formica counters an approving glance, but the unstocked interior of the refrigerator brought forth a thoughtful frown. Maria had left only a quart of milk and a stale piece of cheese to ward off starvation.

Nicola made her way on to the dining room, stopping to replace the candles and silver candleholders on a polished walnut dining table. There was an eggshell-colored rug on the floor, and green floor-to-ceiling draw draperies at the big window on one wall. A walnut buffet with a silver-trimmed tantalus atop it was against the other wall. Thankfully, the oak stand of the tantalus, which enclosed cut-glass decanters, had proved beyond Ivan's talents.

She moved through the archway to the empty living room and admired the grass-cloth walls and white rug, which made such a pleasant background for the green-and-white uphol- stered furniture. The honey shades of the pro- vincial end tables echoed the subdued trend of the apartment's decor. Even though night was falling fast beyond the big sliding window which led to the lanai, Nicola could visualize how well the colors would complement the sunny San Diego climate. She took another look at the plump cushions backing the davenport and conquered an inclination to sink in its oversized depths. From the raised voices down the bedroom hall, it sounded as if Juliette was staging a violent temper tantrum, and Nicola hurried toward the disturbance, wishing she could incarcerate the model as effectively as Ivan.

She opened the first door on her left and lingered on the threshold as she saw the contents of their luggage strewn over the top of a queen-sized bed. Alex's precious fishing rods were tumbled out of their cases beside it.

Juliette's angry voice coming from the room across the hall made her decide that there were more important things than restoring order. She hesitated a minute longer before going over to knock on the door and open it.

Juliette was sitting on the end of the single bed which occupied most of a small but elegant guest room. She had her legs crossed, and her arms were folded defiantly over her breasts as she scowled at Alex, lounging against a nearby dressing table. The sound of the opening door made her pause to give Nicola a negligent glance before turning back to him.

If the sudden appearance of his bride enchanted him, Alex kept it well hidden. He simply sighed and stood up, saying, "I wondered where you'd gotten to."

Nicola wanted to ask why he didn't come and find out. Instead she said mildly, "I think you should lie down and rest that foot for a while." A smile lightened her features. "Of course, it's a little hard to find a bed . . . Ivan's occupying the one in Maria's room . ., and the other bedroom looks as if the East German border guards got to it first."

"We can't touch that stuff until somebody arrives from the police department and takes a report," Alex replied. "Graham said he'd bring them up when they came."

Nicola blinked and looked around. "I wondered where he'd gone."

"Not far," Alex said, sounding as if he wished differently.

"That only leaves one other bed, but you're welcome to it, Alex," Juliette said, patting the mattress beside her. "Temporarily, of course. I'm afraid I'll have to use it tonight." She glanced toward Nicola. "That's what Alex and I were arguing about."

"I merely suggested that I thought you'd be more comfortable over at the hotel tonight," he said. "Frankly, I'm beat . . . and Nicola feels as if she's been on a round-the-world trip rather than a cross-country one."

Juliette directed a clinical look at Nicola's complexion. "You shouldn't have tried to do Tijuana your first day."

"Oh, well, you know women and shopping," Alex cut in before Nicola could declare that she wasn't the one who picked the Mexican detour. "Isn't that right, darling?" he prompted.

"Oh, absolutely," Nicola replied obediently, deciding there were more important things to discuss. "Did you say that you're going to spend the night with us?" she asked, turning back to Juliette.

The model shrugged. "It would be hard to

do anything else today. I left this phone number with my agency, and it's too late to change it. I'll move into another apartment tomorrow, as soon as Kevin makes sure everything is in order."

Nicola managed to keep a bland look on her features as she inquired, "An apartment in this building?"

"Of course," Juliette's eyes widened with well-feigned surprise. "Didn't Alex tell you? Since I'll be working here on his assignment, I thought I might as well enjoy some sunshine before going back to New York. I was able to rent an apartment on the floor below this."

"That *is* handy," Nicola commented without expression. She was deciding the newest development wasn't all bad; having Juliette in the apartment overnight certainly prevented any embarrassing confrontations with Alex. A marriage license might spell respectability to onlookers, but Nicola would have felt a lot surer of her ground if they were simply on the old employer-secretary relationship. "Naturally, Alex and I are delighted to have you spend the night," she announced, keeping her glance fixedly on Juliette. "The only thing is that he should have a bed to himself, with his ankle the way it is. The doctor insisted on complete rest for the next week. But it doesn't matter—I can sleep on the couch for one night."

"Darling, don't be silly!" Alex came alive at that and walked over to put his arm around her shoulders. "I won't think of it. There's plenty of room in that other bed." He was edging her toward the hall door as he spoke. "Right now, Juliette needs some linen to make up her bed, and after the police come to file a report . . . you can straighten things in the other room."

Juliette stood up and stretched like a sleek tigress. "That's fine with me, except you haven't said anything about dinner."

Nicola found herself on the defensive. "There isn't anything in the refrigerator except milk and cheese."

"Obviously we'll have to go out," Juliette concluded.

Her arbitrary decisions were beginning to wear on Nicola. "I'm not very hungry," she had just started to say, when the doorbell interrupted her.

"That must be the police." Alex began limping down the hallway. "Nicola, call the hotel and make a dinner reservation for the three of us in an hour from now. And for Pete's sake, see if you can make that cat be quiet. I can hear him yowling from here."

At that moment, Nicola had a great desire to start yowling alongside Ivan. With both Alex and Juliette issuing orders, she felt like a battered punching bag. It was only Alex's quick reappearance with a uniformed policeman in tow that kept her on an even keel. She nodded courteously at his introduction, and when the policeman announced there was no reason why

Mrs. Laird should be inconvenienced any further, she heaved a sigh of relief. Then he asked smoothly if she would mind taking a quick look through her luggage to see what was missing before he asked Mr. Laird the necessary questions.

Nicola obediently trailed them into the bedroom and started searching through her opened suitcases. A few minutes later she shook her head and reported, "Nothing's missing that I can see. Even my jewel case is still intact." She indicated a suede pouch left prominently on a pile of lingerie.

"Thanks, that's what I wanted to know." Since the officer was opening the bedroom door for her as he spoke, Nicola simply nodded and edged past him.

Ivan's yowls of protest from the storage room were increasing in volume. Nicola noticed that Juliette had cleverly closed her bedroom door to muffle the sound. For an instant she wished she could use the same tactics, until her sympathy for the kitten triumphed.

All that she could find to satisfy his hunger was some instant oatmeal and a can of corned beef in the cupboard. She combined the two in a shallow dish and pointed Ivan in the right direction. Sometime during the kitten's dinner she heard the front door open and close but by then she was using the tiny bath off the kitchen to redo her makeup and comb her hair. Ivan eventually stumbled in to watch her. He was purring loudly—his midsection so rounded that he had trouble reaching over it to lick his paws.

Nicola tickled him behind the ears and went into the living room to sit down before she fell asleep standing up.

She had just sunk into a corner of the couch and was closing her eyes when Alex and Juliette appeared from the bedroom hall.

"Ready to go?" Alex wanted to know. "There should be time for a drink before dinner if we leave now." He frowned at her stricken expression. "What's the matter? Did you have trouble getting the reservation?"

Nicola decided honesty was the best policy. "I forgot all about it. I fed the cat instead."

"There must be some logic to that, but I'm darned if I can see what it is," he said, starting toward the telephone.

Juliette was arranging a black fur-collared sweater over her shoulders. "If you have any trouble, just mention my name. I've practically grown up around here," she went on to explain in kindly fashion to Nicola.

The other could only nod, wishing that she had changed her clothes as well as her makeup. Juliette's black silk sheath did wonders for her high-fashion figure, and her evening sweater was the last word in designer *couture*.

Nicola was trying to smooth the wrinkles from her own outfit when Alex turned from the phone and said, "C'mon, there's no problem.

We can have a drink at the table if we want."
He saw the dubious expression on Nicola's face
and added firmly, "You look fine—stop worry-
ing. Now, for lord's sake, let's go eat."

When they emerged from the elevator in the
lobby, Kevin Graham gave them a morose
greeting. "I talked to that policeman when he
came down. He'll put in a routine report, but
frankly, if our security men can't turn up any
leads, there isn't much hope of nailing anybody."

"Exactly what he told me," Alex said. "All
they have is a breaking-and-entering charge
anyway. Nothing of ours was taken."

"Ivan the Terrible is on guard while we eat,"
Juliette announced, moving over to smooth
Kevin's lapel. "We're just going next door
. . . why don't you join us? I hate uneven
numbers."

"Sorry." The manager's height made it possible for him to smile down at her. "I wish I
could, but I have an early date tomorrow. Another time, maybe."

"Looks as if you're stuck with us," Alex told
Juliette as he reached past her to push open the
glass door. "See you later, Graham."

They were halfway through their dinner in
the famous hotel dining room before the building manager's name came up again. The model
was telling Alex about places to see in the San
Diego area and mentioned how she and Kevin

had gone to the same schools there before she'd deserted California for the more lucrative modeling scene in New York.

"I figured he must be an old friend from the way he turned you down tonight," Alex commented idly. "You don't usually have any trouble finding a man to pick up your dinner checks in Manhattan."

Juliette toyed with some lettuce on her salad plate. "If I know Kevin, his early date means a fishing trip. He's just like you," she told him, "anything with fins comes first."

"Not always." Alex looked amused. "Nicola can testify to that. She caught me in a weak moment at the end of the season. Isn't that right, darling?"

Nicola, who was lost in a reverie of her own, heard only the last part of the sentence. "I beg your pardon?"

"It wasn't important." Alex gave her a crooked smile. "Better have another cup of coffee, or you'll fall asleep sitting there."

She straightened her shoulders. "I wasn't sleepy . . . I was just thinking that a lot's happened since we had brunch in here this morning."

"Well, there's no point in wasting any time when we're on a vacation," Alex said, deliberately misunderstanding her. "Tomorrow, I'm starting you back to work."

Juliette was listening closely. "You're not

talking about a shooting schedule for a day or so, are you?"

"Not until we get some decent props. That's Nicola's department. We could use a Mexican flavor for the lanai background."

Juliette turned to Nicola. "Old Town is your best bet for that. There are some good Mexican gift shops there, and lots of Southwest decor."

"I've read about it," Nicola said. "I thought perhaps Alex could use the zoo for another sequence, or maybe the wild-animal park out at San Pasqual."

"We might drive out there tomorrow if the weather's decent," he cut in.

"I thought you weren't going to stir off the davenport for a while," Juliette reproved.

Nicola, who had thought the same thing, simply stared at him. Her eyes dropped finally before his amused gaze. "You'd better wait and see how you feel," she told him weakly. Even as she said it, she was wondering what had prompted his remark. Alex never had evinced any interest in the preparation work before. Surely a Mexican marriage couldn't have changed him *that* much.

Alex leaned forward to pour more coffee for her. "I meant to tell you—I called William while I was changing and gave him all the news. He sent his best to you."

"That was kind of him." Nicola swallowed, wishing it wasn't so hard to carry on a conversation that made sense to Juliette while Alex was blithely carrying on another dialogue entirely. She was relieved to suddenly see a familiar figure approaching their table. "We weren't the only ones to choose this place to eat," she told Alex. "Isn't that your charter-boat captain coming this way?"

Alex turned to look, and then got to his feet. "I didn't think we'd see you again quite so soon, Pat. You met my wife . . ."

"I sure did." The tall fair-haired man had changed to slacks and a sport coat since the afternoon. "Nice to see you again, Nikki."

Alex's mouth tightened slightly at the other's mode of address, but that was the only outward sign of his annoyance. "Juliette, may I present Pat Towne. He's captain of that charter boat I was on last night. Pat, this is Miss Denver."

"An old friend of Alex's from New York," Juliette added, visibly perking up at the sign of so much masculinity.

"My, my!" Towne made no attempt to hide his admiration. "I can see that I've been in the wrong business all this time. Hope you're staying around, Miss Denver."

"I have every intention of it."

"Good!" He turned back to Alex. "I'm sorry to interrupt, but I was just over at your apartment building, and they told me you were eating here."

"No problem." Alex made a courteous gesture. "Will you join us?"

"No, thanks. I'd like to, but I have an appointment." Patrick's tone became businesslike. "I've just had a cancellation tomorrow afternoon. Thought you might like to have the time. It can be an overnight, if you'd like."

"Alex, darling, you can't," Juliette protested. "You promised to spend the day with Nicola. Surely you aren't going to make her take second place to some silly fishing trip?"

"That's ridiculous!" Nicola cut in before Alex was forced to rescue her. "I think a fishing trip makes more sense than wandering about the countryside with a sprained ankle. Presuming you don't have to walk around to catch fish."

Patrick's tone was solemn, although his eyes gleamed with laughter. "I do my best to make the fish come to him, ma'am."

"Then there's no problem." If she'd been honest, Nicola would have confessed that she was considerably more concerned just then about the night ahead rather than what was going to happen the next day. The fine print of the Mexican marriage license in Alex's possession was looking larger and larger on her horizon.

"Whenever you-all get through making up my mind, just let me know, will you?" There was a cutting edge to Alex's voice.

Nicola could feel a flush creeping up her cheekbones. "I'm sorry, but somebody has to make you follow the doctor's orders."

"You sound just like every other wife I've run into," Patrick assured her with a grin. "As if making decisions for their husbands is guaranteed in the Bill of Rights."

"Okay, I'll go fishing with you, Pat," Alex interrupted. "What time shall I be at the pier?"

"Anytime after noon. I'll see you then." The fishing captain nodded to Nicola and turned to say, "Nice to have met you, Miss Denver," before threading his way out of the dining room.

"Too bad I didn't know he was coming—I could have given him that book on Chapultepec tonight," Alex said, putting his napkin on the table and signaling for the check. "I'll have to try to remember it tomorrow."

Nicola noticed that he made no mention of Pat Towne's invitation that she be included on a fishing trip. Which was just as well, she told herself, and reached down to retrieve her purse from beside her chair.

Juliette's mind was occupied with something else. "What does a fishing-boat captain want with a book on Chapultepec? He must have Mexico City confused with Puerto Vallarta."

"Not necessarily," Alex said calmly. "I found out last night that Pat's a history buff . . . quite an authority on Mexican happenings from the earliest days. He knew all about Maximilian and Carlota's reign."

"Practically everybody knows about them," Juliette sniffed.

"If I remember, you were pretty hazy about events until you read the guidebooks last week."

Nicola felt it was time to intervene before Juliette started raising her voice. "As a matter of fact, I'd enjoy reading your book after Captain Towne is finished," she said. "All I remember about that period was that the Empress went insane when she couldn't get help in Europe for their monarchy, and Maximilian's famous speech when he went before the firing squad. Apparently he dispensed gold pieces and told the soldiers that he forgave them at the same time—just like a movie script."

"Carlota wouldn't have done that," Juliette said. "She was the strong one in that twosome. Even when things were at their worst, she traveled to the coast with a platoon of servants as well as trunks full of clothes and a fabulous collection of jewels."

"Which didn't endear her to the peasants along the way," Alex commented.

Juliette shrugged. "You're probably right. What kind of a book did you bring back from Mexico City?"

"Nothing important. Just one a friend lent me when he heard that I was taking pictures at Chapultepec."

"I should think all the important reference works would be in Spanish."

"Probably they are. This was merely a collection of notes published in London. They're supposed to have been gathered by one of Carlota's diplomatic advisers who accompanied her when she tried to get help from Napoleon III. It's not very exciting reading." Alex pushed back his chair and stood up. "Let's get going, shall we? I can tell you one thing," he continued, trying to smother a yawn as they made their way through the hotel lobby, "I'm certainly not going to read any Mexican history tonight."

Nicola saw her chance. "Then you won't mind if I borrow it?" She kept her voice guileless. "You've got me curious after all this discussion. And tonight looks like my best chance if you're going to lend it to Captain Towne tomorrow."

Alex gave her a sharp look, from which all vestiges of weariness had fled. "I thought you were tired. You said you were tired earlier."

"Well, I'm not tired now," Nicola told him just as definitely.

Juliette leaned forward to watch the interchange with enjoyment. Both Nicola and Alex became aware of her avid expression simultaneously.

"We'll discuss it later," Alex told Nicola, and caught her elbow in a firm grip that discouraged conversation as they started back to the apartment.

Juliette's voice was bland when she pressed

close to his other side. "If I can help in any way, just let me know, Alex dear. I'm available at all hours, and heaven knows . . . it wouldn't be the first time."

5

"Just what did she mean by that?" Nicola hissed angrily when she and Alex were back in the master bedroom of the apartment with the door shut safely behind them.

"What are you talking about?"

Nicola waggled an accusing finger in the direction of the hall. "What Juliette said . . . about it not being the first time she was available." Her eyes narrowed as she watched him sit down on the side of the wide bed. "You seem to be taking it very casually."

"If you expect a reasonable explanation for anything that Juliette says, you've come to the wrong boy." Alex bent down to unlace his shoe. "The Russians should put her on the payroll—she could stir up a minor revolution in the time it takes for a football huddle. It's a good thing she photographs like a dream or she'd have been out of work long ago." He stood up and limped over to his suitcase on a rack by the bathroom door. "Where in the devil are my pajamas?"

Nicola felt things were getting rapidly out of hand. She took a step to follow him. "What do you mean? You can't honestly believe that we're going to share this room."

"It's the only sensible thing to do," Alex growled over his shoulder as he pawed through his belongings. "I should have unpacked this stuff earlier. If you find time tomorrow, maybe you can do it. Incidentally, there are some shirts that should be sent out."

"I am *not* concerned about your laundry," she said, emphasizing the negative.

"I am. There wasn't time to send it out in Mexico City, and if something isn't done pretty soon—"

"That's not the point," she cut in, coming over beside him. "I mean that I can handle the laundry problem, but this bedroom situation is something I didn't bargain for." She decided to abandon diplomacy in favor of straightforward speaking. "There was nothing in that list of rules for Mexican marriages that said anything about sharing the same bed. You can just go in there and tell Juliette that . . . that . . ."

"Tell her what?" Alex straightened with a pair of pajamas in his hands and watched her flounder for the proper word. "Exactly," he concluded when the pause lengthened. "That's the problem. So we're not telling Juliette anything. Good God, Nicola . . . there's no need for you to start acting like a scared Victorian parlor maid. That bed's big enough for a family of circus acrobats, so you shouldn't have any trouble staying out of my clutches. And frankly, I'm too damned tired to chase you around it." He tossed his pajamas on the bureau and started to loosen his tie.

Nicola's panic increased as she saw his dogged expression. She'd learned long ago that it was useless to try to change his mind when he looked like that. On the other hand, she had no intention of compromising her own principles. At least until she was sure that there wasn't an alternative.

Alex was calmly unbuttoning his shirt by then. Almost daring her to object, she thought, as her glance went around the room, searching for a last-minute reprieve. Suddenly she saw a thin volume entitled *Maximilian and Carlota* on the end of the dressing table and hurried over to pick it up. "I can read," she said, turning back to Alex triumphantly. "That's what I can do."

He looked up from removing a cufflink to stare at her. "Congratulations! Somehow I just took it for granted all this time."

"No . . ." Her lips tightened in annoyance. "I mean I can read tonight." She sidled toward the door, leaving plenty of space between them. "I can read this book in the living room, and if Juliette comes out and gets curious, I'll just say that I didn't want to disturb your rest by keeping the bedroom light on." She paused with one hand on the knob and smiled at him. "Sleep well—I hope your ankle doesn't bother you."

His return glance was sharp, but his voice didn't give anything away as he said, "I don't expect *that* to bother me at all."

Nicola managed to close the door behind her and get halfway down the hall toward the living room while she considered his last comment. Then she shrugged and told herself she was imagining things. Alex wasn't a man to go in for hidden meanings; probably he was secretly relieved that she'd left him in peace. She only wished that the thought of spending the night on the couch in her clothes was as appealing.

She moved on out to the living room and put her book on an end table while she assessed the davenport as a makeshift bed. It was long enough, but the bottom cushions were firm and boxlike rather than the yielding variety. Perhaps borrowing some of the small decorative throw pillows from the chairs might help. It wouldn't do to make permanent-looking arrangements until Juliette was positively settled for the night in her bedroom. Even after that, Nicola decided she'd have to sleep with one eye open so that she could escape back into the master bedroom before the model stirred in the morning.

She sat down on the davenport and opened the slim volume which told the saga of Maximilian and his unfortunate bride.

In the next half-hour Nicola learned a great deal about the brief reign of the Hapsburg emperor in the New World. She also learned that she wouldn't have any trouble waking up early in the morning, because it was doubtful that she'd close an eye in the interim. By then the davenport cushions felt as if they were stuffed with sawdust shavings, and if that weren't enough, Ivan had started to protest his fate in the utility room. His howls of anguish were remarkable considering his size, and they increased as the time passed. Nicola expected that either Alex or Juliette would arrive momentarily to comment on the racket, but either they were sound sleepers or Ivan's range didn't reach to the end of the hallway.

Unfortunately, his yowling could be heard loud and clear in the living room, and even the book's account of Carlota's jewels couldn't hold Nicola's attention. When she found herself reading about the Empress's jeweled water-lily brooch for the third time, she decided that Ivan had won.

She swung her feet to the floor and stood up, putting the book on the end table until she returned.

Ivan greeted her from the top of a carton in the utility room. He scrambled down to the floor, but he didn't miss a single meow of protest on the way. It wasn't until Nicola picked him up and cuddled his warm little body against her breast that the yowls stopped and were replaced by a purring so loud that it rocked his rib cage.

"Ivan . . . you're terrible! What in the world's wrong with you?" Since she was stroking the miscreant's ears at the time, the admonition didn't disturb him. "You must be hungry again," Nicola went on in a soft monotone as his unblinking amber eyes watched her. "It would have been nice if Maria had left a note or a can of cat food somewhere," she continued conversationally as she moved over to the kitchen cupboards and started opening them with her free hand.

Unfortunately, a search of the premises didn't reveal any new treasures, so she shook her head and reached for the instant oatmeal once again. "Sorry, Ivan. At least this should fill you up for a little while, and tomorrow I promise to go shopping. Either that, or Maria will be back to take charge. Now, if you'll just sit on the floor and wait until I heat some milk for this . . ."

The instant Ivan's pink pads touched the linoleum, he resumed his objections—loudly. He wasn't keen on oatmeal, he didn't approve of the cold floor, and he most certainly didn't intend to be ignored any longer.

However, when his hastily prepared dinner was put in front of him, he allowed himself to be diverted, and Nicola found herself wishing that her thoughts could be channeled as easily.

Even though Alex was out of her sight, he

certainly wasn't out of her mind, and she was finding that a wedding ceremony, no matter how platonic, aroused some desires that she'd thought were safely buried.

She stared down at Ivan's furry back as he crouched over a Wedgewood saucer, wondering if Alex would be tempted by Juliette's recent invitation. Then she shook her head in disgust. Alex wouldn't commit such a gaffe—not when his in-name-only wife was sitting in the living room. For an instant she debated whether Juliette had issued a similar invitation in Mexico City, and felt a leaden reaction in her stomach. Exactly the kind Ivan was going to have if he didn't stop gulping down his oatmeal.

She picked up the little tiger cat after he'd turned away from the polished saucer and transported him back to the utility room. He allowed her to close the door when he sleepily arched his back and started a spit-and-polish operation on his paws.

The saga of Maximilian and Carlota didn't seem nearly as appealing when Nicola opened the book a second time. There were some rough drawings of the royal jewels before the biographer recounted the Empress's final journey overland in 1866. He included graphic descriptions of muddy roads and soggy stopovers on the way to Veracruz, where Carlota was finally able to set sail for Europe.

At that point, Nicola glanced around at the austere furnishings in the apartment and shivered, wondering if Carlota had thought to take a blanket on *her* hurried exodus.

She sighed and concentrated on the book again, forcing herself to read on. The next pages contained rough facsimiles of love letters exchanged between the royal couple during their separation. Carlota's impassioned declaration to her husband which said "I am clinging to you from the depths of my soul" succeeded in making Nicola stir restlessly on her couch.

For the first time, she admitted to herself that she wasn't merely cold; she was lonely. And, unlike Ivan, her loneliness couldn't be helped by a dish of lukewarm oatmeal.

Nicola's eyes grew bleak as she dwelled on that truth at some length, the book momentarily forgotten in her grasp. It was all very well for Carlota to proclaim her love to the skies . . . quite another thing for hapless females of the next generation.

For the umpteenth time since the trip to Tijuana, Nicola shook her head disconsolately. She'd been a fool to listen to Alex; the sooner she extricated herself from this embarrassing situation, the better.

That decision eased her mental state, but it didn't help her physical situation. Cold air seeping around the the edges of the glass lanai door made her sneeze sharply. The noise of the sneeze evidently carried to the utility room, because there were a couple of tentative meows from Ivan before he gave up and fell asleep again. Lucky Ivan, Nicola thought dismally, wishing she'd brought a handkerchief as well as a blanket.

The final chapter of Maximilian's reign did nothing to improve her frame of mind. By the time she read the news of the emperor's capture and arrest, she was ready to weep along with his followers. Tears trickled down her cheeks at the account of his last day, when he proclaimed, "I pardon everyone and pray that all pardon me. I hope that my blood flows for the good of this earth."

Her tears increased as she went on to read how the Austrian had looked up at the sky on the morning of his execution and remarked, "What a glorious day! I could not have chosen a better one on which to die!"

Nicola closed the book with a snap and dropped it on the end table. What a story to be reading on her wedding night! All she needed was a record of the "Funeral March" from Saul to complete the misery.

She stood up, snapped off the reading light, and headed for the hallway. How ridiculous to be getting chilblains in the living room when there was a perfectly good mattress and wool blankets going begging in the bedroom. If she persisted in acting like a Jane Austen heroine, the only tangible results would be a sore throat and sniffles in the morning. And if Alex Laird had any other ideas about her return, she'd soon put him straight.

Nicola was so fired up with determination when she stormed into the bedroom that Alex's still figure stretched out on the side of the bed was almost disappointing. She stared at him suspiciously and listened to his deep, even breathing before concluding that her husband (in name only) had absolutely nothing on his mind just then.

Closing the door quietly behind her, she tiptoed across the bedroom. She slipped out of her shoes and momentarily considered getting into a nightgown and robe, then discarded the idea. Instead she merely undressed down to her slip and piled her things on her unpacked suitcase. Then she moved over to the bed, where she managed to retrieve the down comforter which Alex had carelessly kicked aside. All she wanted just then was to wrap herself in its warm cocoon and lay her head on the unused pillow which Alex had also pushed out of his way.

It didn't take long for Nicola to do just that. Her careful movements apparently did nothing to disturb the deep slumber of the man at her side; he sighed once, and then, while Nicola remained frozen, turned more comfortably on his stomach and relaxed again.

Nicola took a moment to congratulate herself on her "better-late-than-never" decision and set her mental alarm early so that she'd be off the bed by the time Alex woke up. Then she unconsciously echoed his comfortable sigh and fell soundly asleep.

Her slumber was so deep that she was only vaguely aware of an annoying distraction later on. She came partially awake to realize her shoulder was being shaken and Alex was complaining.

"For Pete's sake, Nicola . . . wake up, will you! Anybody would think you'd been out on the tiles all night instead of Ivan."

"Ivan?" Her response was muffled by the pillow. "Who's Ivan?"

"Ivan is the cat who's yowling his head off in the utility room. My God, don't tell me you can't hear him."

Nicola opened her eyes just enough to learn that Alex was standing beside the bed at her side. A glimmer of light coming from the bathroom showed that he'd donned a robe, but that was all he'd managed in the way of amenities. He was heavy-eyed and raking his fingers through his tousled hair as he waited for her answer.

"Can't you do something about it?" he persisted when her eyelids started down again.

"Do somethin' 'bout what?" Nicola asked irritably, unable to tune him out.

"Ivan. I-v-a-n. The cat. Remember?" Alex bent over to give her another shake.

"Go 'way." Nicola fumbled for the blanket to get out of reach. "You feed him. *I* fed him earlier."

"What does he eat? Nicola . . . *will* you wake up?"

"No." She burrowed into the pillow and then relented. "Oatmeal. It's in the cupboard—I think." The last two words were tacked on after he moved across the room and the door closed none too softly behind him. Nicola thumped her pillow into a comfortable position and promptly went back to sleep.

When she awoke the next time, it was because she had decided it was no use trying to sleep in a sawmill. She opened her eyes just enough to identify sunlight streaming around the draw drapes at the bedroom windows, and duly noted that it wasn't the middle of the night, as she'd suspected. The constant rumble of noise still distracted her, and her eyelids went up a little more, enough for her to recognize a dark head inches away. Satisfied that she'd located the trouble, she let her lashes go back down again. Four seconds later, she sat bolt upright as the double-take registered. "Good lord!"

Her exclamation was enough to make Alex open his eyes, rub his bristly chin, and say irritably, "Give back the blanket—it's colder than hell in here."

Stricken, Nicola looked down and saw that she had indeed removed most of the covering from his long form. The blanket that she'd claimed as her sole property, in the middle of the night had somehow become community property, with both of them huddled under it. She hastily relinquished enough to cover an expanse of male chest and dark blue pajama bottoms. Apparently the sheet had disappeared earlier in the confusion. Then she realized that the lacy top of her slip was letting in a draft, and she slid back down under a corner of the comforter. "I didn't mean to take all the covers. You woke me up . . . rumbling like that."

"I don't rumble. Snore maybe . . . but not rumble." He yawned and considered it. "You heard Ivan."

"Ivan!" For a moment, panic made her forget everything. "You mean he was in this bed."

"He still is." Alex went on irritably, "Will you stop flouncing around and letting in all that cold air? Now, look"—his grumble became accusing—"You've woke him up. Well, you can get him back to sleep this time. I've spent half the night working at it."

As if waiting for his entrance cue, young Ivan emerged from the comforter and staggered toward the headboard, licking his pink nose as he came.

"Exactly what," Nicola demanded of the back of Alex's head, "is that kitten doing here?"

Alex turned back to survey her balefully. Even the appearance of Ivan settling into the comforter between them did nothing to appease him. "The cat's here because he didn't like oatmeal at three o'clock in the morning. I wasn't crazy about it myself when I walked barefooted into the dish of it you'd left on the kitchen floor."

She winced and said automatically, "I'm sorry, I had some left over and didn't know what else to do with it."

"I gathered that. Ivan also made it clear that he didn't care for the utility room any longer." Alex stopped to rub the side of his nose. "Actually, I can't say that I blame him. But by that time, both of us were tired of discussing things on the linoleum. He settled down like a perfect gentleman when I brought him in here. The only one I had trouble with was you."

Nicola's lips parted. "Me?" she squeaked.

"You," he confirmed. "You have a distressing tendency to sleep on the diagonal, and it was a little hard on Ivan and me—even on a mattress this size. But we managed to work it out."

There was no disguising his amusement at her flushed cheeks. She said through clenched teeth, "I'm terribly sorry to have disturbed you ... both. If you'll excuse me ..."

"Don't go—unless you're thinking of getting breakfast." Alex was squinting at his watch. "It's still fairly early, but I could use some coffee."

"Is that a suggestion or an order?" she asked, drawing up the comforter like a bastion between them. Ivan, deprived of his warm niche, protested in familiar tones.

"Good God, don't start him off again," Alex warned, putting a protective arm around the kitten.

"He's probably just hungry. It's no wonder . . . the poor thing can't live on oatmeal. You'll have to go to the grocery."

"He might be tempted with coffee in the meantime." Alex punched his pillow up under his head and allowed the kitten to curl at his side. "Call us when things are ready. You can have first shift in the bathroom."

As his eyes closed, Nicola was tempted to administer a swift poke where it would do the most good. She was also about to mention that cooking breakfast wasn't part of a secretary's duties when it occurred to her that it certainly was one of the wifely ones. Alex wouldn't hesitate to announce it.

His eyelids opened a slit as she lingered. "Are you going?"

Nicola sighed, knowing she was defeated. "I guess so."

"Umm." A satisfied murmur came from his throat. Then, as she stood up, he added, "You'd better wake up Juliette, too. Pound on the door when you go past."

"For breakfast, you mean?" Her query wasn't enthusiastic.

"Among other things. Frankly, the sooner she moves into her own apartment, the better."

Nicola contented herself with a noncommittal murmur. She stood up and walked across the room to her suitcase, hoping that Alex was dozing rather than inspecting her appearance. His earlier expression showed that he'd been amused by her choice of nightwear, but thankfully he hadn't said anything about it.

She resisted an urge to look over her shoulder, and kept her movements unhurried as she opened her small suitcase on top of the dressing table.

"I'm sorry that your belongings are such a mess." Alex's calm tone showed that he wasn't missing a bit of the action. "There wasn't time to sort things out last night after that policeman came," he went on easily. "I just shoved everything back in afterward."

"It doesn't matter." By then Nicola had located her aqua-and-white travel robe and pulled it on, tying the bow at her throat with fingers that trembled despite her efforts to appear casual. It was all very well for Alex to stretch out in bed revealing a breadth of tanned chest as he discussed the local crime rate, but she found it difficult to match his nonchalance.

Once Nicola was clad, she did better. She even managed to comb her hair under his interested masculine gaze and then spent some time selecting a pale blue blouse and skirt with patchwork pockets to take into the bathroom with her. "I'll unpack the rest after breakfast," she said airily.

"What then?"

Her eyebrows went up at his query. "I suppose I'd better make a search this forenoon for those props. Old Town might be best for piñatas, too. They should be good if you want a patio shot."

He frowned slightly. "I wish I hadn't promised that job so soon. The idea of relaxing in the sunshine is a lot more appealing." A plaintive meow from the folds of the comforter reminded him of something else. "And don't forget to buy some food. Otherwise, Ivan will be running away from home . . . or I will."

"It's a good thing you have that ankle for an excuse, and that you're still paying me a salary—" she began, when he interrupted her ruthlessly.

"What salary? Whoever heard of a wife getting a salary?" He sat up and shoved aside the covers. "Where in the devil's my robe?"

She retrieved it from the foot of the bed and gave it to him, watching as he thrust an arm in the sleeve. "If my salary stopped yesterday afternoon," she continued in a level tone, "then I'd better write home for money."

Alex stood up and belted the robe. "What's wrong with my money?"

"Not a thing. Except that it's yours."

"All right . . . an allowance, then, if you're being technical. You've been writing checks on that bank account for years—why is it different now?"

"Because then I worked for my salary. You know perfectly well that fixing breakfast isn't the same thing at all."

"There will be other things you can do."

Nicola started to ask just what he meant by that, but there was something in his glance that made her decide against it. She picked up her clothes and fled to the bathroom without saying another word.

Feminine pride kept her going for the next hour. Alex made his vacation status official by wearing jeans and a comfortable denim shirt when he appeared at breakfast. There was no more discussion about duties as he consumed toast and coffee and supervised Ivan when the kitten tried some shavings of cheese. Juliette didn't enter the kitchen until Nicola was putting on a cardigan and getting ready to leave.

"Where are you off to?" the model wanted to know.

"Shopping," Nicola replied, trying to sound enthusiastic about the prospect. "There's coffee on the stove, and bread in the drawer, if you're hungry."

"You don't have to tell me. I was the one who put them there." Juliette's smooth brow creased. "Where's Alex?"

"On the lanai, the last time I looked. He's the one stretched out on the chaise longue next to the cat."

Juliette frowned at the mention of Maria's legacy. "Something will have to be done about that cat. He was making a terrible racket last night."

Nicola thought that Juliette could have taken measures at the time rather than waiting twelve hours to complain, even as she replied that Ivan was in a better mood at the moment.

"I'm glad of that." Juliette smoothed her hair and headed for the lanai. "Don't let me keep you—I'll see if Alex wants more coffee."

She crossed the room like a panther searching for something tasty. A minute later she was bending over Alex's relaxed figure to greet him affectionately. Nicola stayed where she was. A sprained ankle didn't make a man helpless, and his laughter showed that he wasn't suffering as she finally headed for the door. So much for Alex's statement that he wanted Juliette out of the apartment. And so much for Nicola's niggling hope that maybe a license from Tijuana had changed his attitude toward women.

The bright sunshine dappling the lobby of the apartment building raised her spirits as she left the elevator. She returned the smile of the security guard who lingered by a desk in the corner. There was no sign of Kevin Graham, and Nicola pursed her lips thoughtfully before she crossed the condominium's inner patio toward the parking lot. The building manager was pleasantly uncomplicated, and he had shown more warmth toward her the day before than was strictly necessary. Besides, it wouldn't hurt Alex to see that not all men preferred statuesque brunettes.

Nicola didn't have a chance to linger on that train of thought, because she discovered a Coronado supermarket a few blocks away and

parked in front of it. It was time for Ivan to be
introduced to the wonders of the pet-food department. She emerged a half-hour later, laden
with brown paper bags and the comforting
knowledge that none of them would face starvation in the immediate future. By then she was
transformed into an eager tourist who checked
a city map for directions before driving toward
the graceful arch of the Coronado Bridge.

Despite the gradual improvement in the
weather, the waters of the bay beneath the steel
span looked as gray as the paint on a naval patrol craft which was just then heading toward a
mooring farther south. Nicola brought her attention quickly back to the traffic ahead of her
and a few minutes later took the bridge exit
which led to the center of town. When she
reached the main San Diego business district,
the sunshine had increased—enough so that she
lowered her car window while waiting for a
traffic light beside Horton Plaza. There was a
champagne sparkle to the gentle breeze that
swept through the car, and as she drove on, the
tops of the towering office buildings looked like
white cardboard cutouts against the sky.

There was nothing even approaching their
contemporary facades when she finally parked
the car at the edge of Old Town and started
strolling past its picturesque buildings. Adobe
faces had replaced stark concrete on the district's old homes, and the commercial section

showed a south-of-the-border air with tiled inner patios and roofs.

Nicola decided to enjoy her stay and wandered through the various museums before sitting down to buy a cup of coffee and checking her shopping list. Alex needed piñatas, two outsize ceramic candelabra, and an embroidered wedding shirt for a male model in addition to some large terra-cotta containers. Nicola decided that it would be easiest to buy the empty flowerpots at the Mexican garden shop down the block and arrange to have them planted later at the Coronado nursery near the apartment. The rest of the items should be easily available at the large gift shop just across the street from where she was sitting.

She wandered over a few minutes later and stood in the front patio admiring their piñata display. In view of the season, they featured Halloween piñatas with purple-faced witches scowling atop their brooms, and next to them were rows of splendid pumpkin piñatas for more conservative buyers. Nicola had impulsively selected a witch before she remembered that people might stare when she carried it aboard the plane on her trip home. Then she thought of the pleasure she would derive from William's horrified countenance when she appeared with it on East Seventy-second Street. She dwelt for an instant on Alex's more immediate reaction and decided to try her luck. "Put it over there, please," she told the salesclerk.

"I'll take it, but there are some other things I need, too."

She knew instinctively that Alex would be pleased with the rest of her purchases. There was a colorful parrot piñata which would do for photographs in any season, and two ceramic candelabra which were colorful and charming in design. She watched them being carefully packed and resolved to make sure they got back to the East Coast as well. The wedding shirt didn't pose any problems except that most of the sizes were for small men, but the clerk obligingly searched through his stock until he found one that might cover a taller man's shoulders. She doubted that Alex would add the elaborately decorated shirt to his personal wardrobe once the pictures were finished; even the *guayaberra* he'd brought back from a trip to Yucátan had been trimmed with plain buttons rather than the elaborate pearl ones normally shown.

"I guess that's all," Nicola finally told the clerk, and started signing traveler's checks to cover the bill. She gave the young man her car key and arranged for him to put her purchases in the station wagon while she went on down the block to shop for the terra-cotta pots.

The salesman returned the key to her in the garden shop on his way back and assured her that he'd stowed everything carefully and still left enough room for some good-sized flowerpots as well. Nicola thanked him and added a tip which he palmed smoothly while he was still telling her it wasn't necessary.

The garden-shop salesman was so impressed with the maneuver that he quickly volunteered to deliver her new purchases once Nicola had made her selection. Eventually he loaded three of the large planters onto a wheelbarrow and let Nicola carry the brightly painted urn which looked almost Egyptian in design with its tall lines and graceful handles. Nicola wasn't sure that Alex would approve, but there was a chance he would choose it to add interest in the background. The planting used for that particular container would have to be exactly right, Nicola decided. Probably she should consult Alex before she went to the nursery.

As she drove along the arterial which led to the downtown freeway, she winced as she caught a glimpse of her dashboard clock. It was almost half-past twelve, and Alex had wanted to be driven to his fishing junket about then.

If she'd only thought to set a definite time for her return, there wouldn't have been a problem, but Juliette's appearance had made her forget things like civilized farewells and common acts of courtesy.

An automatic glance in the rear-vision mirror showed the purple-faced witch's profile as she rode on her piñata in the back of the station wagon. Nicola smiled as she stared at it a moment longer. Amazing how that purple chin resembled Juliette's!

A little later she drove in the condominium parking lot, stopping as close as she could to the building entrance. She carried an armload of groceries on her first trip up the elevator, and Alex pulled the door open while she was still fumbling at the lock. "Look out . . . the bag's slipping," Nicola gasped as she struggled to hang on to it.

"Give it to me," Alex said tersely. "For Pete's sake, why didn't you ask for some help?"

"Because I didn't think you should be using that ankle to carry things," she said, trailing him into the kitchen and watching him deposit the groceries on the counter.

"It wouldn't have hurt me. Anyway, Juliette could have helped you . . ." he muttered.

"Is she still here?" Nicola tried to sound calmly disinterested, but she must have fallen short, because there was an amused laugh from the dining-room archway, where Juliette lounged.

"Still here, darling. The sunshine felt so good on the lanai that Alex and I couldn't tear ourselves away from it. Did I hear that you needed help with something?"

"Not really. Thanks just the same. The rest of the stuff's a little bulky. Kevin must have someone who can carry it up."

Alex was putting milk in the refrigerator. "Might as well store away the cat food. Maria came back right after you left and took Ivan with her for a couple of days. She thought he might lighten the atmosphere."

"Oh." Nicola was disconcerted at his news; she had looked forward to seeing the tiger kitten again. "Well, he'll probably like a change of scenery."

"I don't know about that. He was raising an unholy racket when she took him away." Alex absently opened a package of snack crackers and sampled one.

"If you'd like, I can heat some soup to go with that, and make a sandwich," Nicola offered.

Alex looked at his watch before shaking his head. "Sounds good, but there isn't time. I'm due on the boat in fifteen minutes. Maybe Juliette would like—"

The model cut in before he could finish. "Juliette's going over to the hotel for lunch, as soon as you leave." Her eyes took on a feline glint as she reported, "I have a better offer."

"Congratulations." Nicola turned to Alex. "I can drive you to the boat now if you're ready...."

"What about *your* lunch?"

"I'm not very hungry," she told him truthfully. "I had coffee while I was in Old Town."

"Okay, then. I'll get my stuff."

Juliette followed him into the hall. "Thanks for carrying my bag to the new apartment."

"No trouble. I'll see you in a day or so. If this

weather holds, we can do some of the outdoor layouts as soon as I get back from this trip."

"You're just going down to Baja?" Juliette probed.

"Probably. Wherever they're biting," he replied.

Both women watched him disappear into the bedroom to get his gear, and then Juliette walked to the front door. "I'll be on my way," she said to Nicola. "I suppose I should thank you for your hospitality last night."

"It isn't necessary. Next time, I hope things won't be in such a muddle," Nicola said, secretly amused. Juliette was finding it difficult to accept the fact that Alex had a wife.

"Well, I'll see you later," Juliette managed, and left without any more amenities.

Nicola had started back to the kitchen when the phone rang. A second peal showed that Alex wasn't answering it on the bedroom extension, so she hurried to lift the receiver on the wall phone by the freezer. "Hello," she said breathlessly.

There was no reply, and without thinking, she repeated more loudly, "Hello."

A low, indistinguishable mutter answered her. The slight frown creasing her forehead deepened as the sinister mutter changed an instant later to low, mocking laughter. And then, as she still gripped the receiver, there came a noisy click as the connection was broken, severing the laughter like a sharp blade.

Nicola slammed down her own receiver with unsteady fingers. She waited for a moment and then cautiously lifted the instrument again, only to hear the monotonous hum of the dial tone.

Alex found her still there when he came through the dining-room door. "I've got my stuff together—we'd better get going . . ." He broke off at the sight of her face. "What's the matter? You look as if you'd seen a ghost!"

Nicola shook her head as if to clear it, and managed a faint smile. "I didn't *see* one. For a minute I thought I'd heard one."

He fell into step beside her. "What are you talking about? Was it somebody we know? Some friend?"

"No." Her expression was solemn as she pulled up and faced him. "That's the only thing I *do* know. He definitely wasn't a friend of ours."

6

"You didn't get enough sleep last night, so I'm not surprised that you're imagining things like threatening phone calls." Alex made his announcement a little later when Nicola was chauffeuring him to the sport-fishing piers by Point Loma. He waited until she turned onto the North Harbor Drive before continuing his lecture. "After staying up half the night, you wrapped yourself like a mummy when you finally did come to bed. What in God's name did you think I was going to do? Bar the door and act like King Kong if you took off your clothes?"

"You needn't exaggerate—"

"Who's exaggerating? You certainly didn't give the impression of a repressed female before this. I don't know why you have to start now."

She shot him an annoyed look. "That's a dubious distinction if I ever heard one. First I'm accused of being a therapy case, and then you tell me that I've behaved like a scarlet woman in the past. You'd better make up your mind."

"That's no problem," he told her coolly. "It's your mind that concerns me at the moment. What makes you think that somebody's signaling you out for obscene phone calls when he didn't say a word? Next thing, my girl, you'll be looking under your bed at night."

"With you around, I'd be far more apt to check what's on top of the mattress," she flared back. "You needn't be so damned patronizing."

"Hey, take it easy." There was laughter in his tone. "Where's your sense of humor?"

"Repressed women don't have one." She braked to let a car cut in front of them for the airport exit and then made an apologetic grimace. "Sorry . . . I guess I am a little edgy lately."

"Maybe you've had cause," Alex allowed magnanimously. "It isn't easy having to cope with a new husband."

"In name only," she put in.

"A new husband," he repeated firmly, taking no notice, "and two overnight guests."

"Two?" Her expression became impish. "Oh, you mean Ivan, as well. I didn't mind him at all."

"That's what I gathered when you introduced me to Juliette's namesake," he replied, jerking his head toward the back of the station wagon, where the purple-faced witch was still astride her broom. "For lord's sake, don't make any Freudian slips like that when our shooting schedule starts. I don't want to have to start interviewing models in San Diego. Incidentally, I like that stuff you brought for props." He waved a hand to encompass her purchases.

"Thanks. I forgot to ask you if it's all right to make arrangements with a nursery for planting the containers."

He half-turned to give them a second glance. "Go ahead. They look fine to me. Have the gardeners put in some wide-leaved tropicals—about the height of the lanai railing. If you find a six-foot-tall ornamental palm in a bamboo tub, ask them to send that along, too." He leaned back to face her again. "And get somebody to help you cart the rest of this stuff up to the apartment."

"All right, I will." She smiled as she turned into the boat basin. "Any other orders while you're gone?"

"I'd tell you to take it easy if I thought it would do any good." He watched her maneuver into a curved drive in front of the charter-boat area and then pull into a handy parking space. "There's Pat's cruiser at that first dock. Damn! I forgot that book I promised him. You'd better come along and soothe his feelings. Grab that case of rods, will you?"

"For a moment, I thought you just wanted my company," she reproved, taking the key out of the ignition and opening her door.

"That, too." Alex loaded a rod case into her

arms and picked up his zipper carryall before leading the way toward a string of power cruisers moored to the long wooden dock.

Nicola was trying to see everything yet avoid tripping over the uneven planks at her feet. "There must be fifty boats in here—are they all for charter?"

"You'll have to ask Pat. He didn't volunteer any information on his competitors—I got the idea that it's 'survival of the fittest' for these fellows."

The tanned captain was waiting to give them a hand as they came aboard, but he wasn't forthcoming with statistics when Nicola quizzed him a few minutes later.

"There are too damned many of us," he admitted. "Especially in the transitional seasons. That's why I can't afford to let any good prospects like Alex here escape from my clutches. You'll notice that I've even made the bunk this time."

"He should be flattered," Nicola commented as she looked in the main cabin with frank curiosity. There was the usual compact galley and eating area at the side, plus two well-worn upholstered benches which obviously converted into extra overnight bunks. The carpeting on the cabin floor was clean but stained and threadbare in one corner, giving the impression that the charter business wasn't lucrative at the moment. Nicola tried to keep her conclusions hidden as she went back to the stern and rejoined the men who were leaning against the waist-high bait box. "I'll go ashore," she told Pat. "I'm sure you want to cast off."

"We should have gone before this," he admitted, with an impatient look at a canvas-covered cart on the dock alongside the ship. "I've been waiting for one of the fellows from the marina to pick that up. The contents have to be delivered when we get back from this trip. They're some Mexican gewgaws my last client brought back from Baja. The only things he managed to carry ashore were his fish. He connected with some nice yellowtail. . . ."

"No kidding." Alex had an intent look. "Wonder if we'll have as much luck?"

"You won't if you don't get going," Nicola said, clambering over the rail and jumping down to the dock. "I can wheel the cart up to the marina for you, Pat. It isn't heavy." She gave it an easy push to illustrate. "I'll give them your instructions, so you won't have to hang around."

"Okay, thanks." Towne grinned in relief. "See you in a day or so," he called as he walked forward toward the flying bridge. "Next time, plan to come along."

Alex still stood at the stern and watched him go. Then he put his hands in the pockets of his cotton slacks and leaned over the rail, saying, "Come back here, Nicola . . . there's something else."

She moved back to the side of the dock and

stood looking at him with concern. "What is it?
Did you forget something important?"

"I think so," Alex said blandly. He bent
down and kissed her thoroughly and possessively on the lips. He took his time about it,
keeping a firm arm around her shoulders.
When he finally released her, Nicola had to
lean against the cruiser's hull to recover her
balance. "That should keep Pat from getting
any wrong ideas," Alex murmured wickedly,
watching her struggle to get her breath back.
"You need more practice, my girl. In the meantime, take care of yourself while I'm gone." He
gave her a careless salute and disappeared in
the cabin.

If there had been anything loose on the dock,
Nicola would have promptly heaved it after
him. That cryptic look showed that he'd carefully gauged the effects of the farewell kiss. His
comprehensive masculine glance had wandered
over her flushed cheeks and trembling fingers
with barely hidden amusement, completely
destroying her try for surface sophistication.

"Damn it to hell!" she muttered as she
shoved the barrow with Pat Towne's cargo
ahead of her up the dock. She deliberately ignored the sound of the twin diesel engines of
the cruiser, determined not to give Alex another chance to score over her. By the time he
returned from Baja, she'd have worked out
some kind of defense against him—even if it involved a letter of resignation and the use of her

return ticket to New York. Which might be the best solution after all, she determined realistically as she struggled to get the cart up the final ramp of the marina. She left it by the side of the building while she went in search of a dock-hand—risking a peek through a corner window once she got inside. Pat's cruiser was already away from the dock and heading for the channel leading to the ocean. Nicola could see the captain's brawny figure up on the bridge, but Alex wasn't in view.

It wasn't surprising, she told herself, as she lingered by the glass. Alex wasn't the type of man to stand on deck gazing soulfully into the distance as he thought about the women in his life. At that moment he was probably checking his tackle box, his mind already on the next day's catch.

As it happened, Nicola was wrong in her gloomy assumption. Alex was even then perched on a leather stool in the forward part of the cabin staring out at the channel, but his thoughts weren't on the marine activity around them. He was thinking of his wife's soft, parted lips and trying to decide why a simple kiss that had been intended solely to remind Nicola of her new role had left him feeling as if he'd been caught in a propeller. He was grateful that the cruiser required all of Pat's attention just then. With any luck, the captain would stay up on the flying bridge and give him time to think.

If he'd followed his natural desires, he'd have ordered Pat to turn around and head back to the marina, where he'd set about convincing Nicola that he didn't have the slightest desire for a "platonic" marriage.

He pictured her trusting face and then winced at the thought of her reaction. Nicola's air of sophistication had never fooled him; indeed, it was her refreshing naiveté which had attracted him in the first place.

Even that simple kiss he'd bestowed a few minutes before had proved that he'd rushed his fences. "I'll be damned lucky if she doesn't leave me flat," Alex muttered, and wanted to slam his fist against the cruiser's control panel in angry frustration. There was only one thing left for him to do: take it slowly and try to recapture the easy relationship he'd engineered in the past. Which was fine, he told himself, except that he didn't want an easy, friendly relationship with his wife. He wanted to take her behind closed doors and make love to her in a way she'd never forget—a way that showed she meant everything in the world to him.

His expression was rueful as he thought about the night they'd spent together. Nicola would never know what an effort it had been for him to stifle his desires. It was just as well that she'd be safely out of reach tonight; his willpower wasn't as strong as he'd thought.

A loud warning blast from a sailboat which was emerging from the yacht-club mooring managed to penetrate his thoughts. Alex gave the craft a casual glance and then turned toward the galley, deciding to drown his gloom with a mug of coffee.

Nicola heard that strident sailboat blast as it carried over the still water to the marina. By then she had found a deckhand who'd reported there wasn't any storage space left in their building. If Captain Towne wanted such facilities, he'd have to make special arrangements with the marina manager, who wasn't available.

Nicola spoiled his lecture when she said that she'd store Captain Towne's belongings, loading them in her station wagon until other arrangements could be made. The deckhand was so surprised that he offered to help in the transfer before remembering that such things weren't part of his duties.

A little later, he watched her drive out of the marina lot in the laden car. It had been a job getting all that Mexican stuff from the cart crammed into the station wagon: aluminum masks and a ceramic washbasin took up room. So did blankets and that oversized flowerpot. He wouldn't spend money on that kind of junk, he thought with a scowl of satisfaction. A cold beer made more sense. He looked at his watch and smiled. What better time than now?

Driving back on the highway leading to Coronado, Nicola was wishing she knew what to do for the rest of her afternoon. A cold beer didn't even figure in the possibilities as she tried to decide how to fill the hours until Alex came back.

By the time Nicola had driven across the long bridge and paid the toll, she'd decided a relaxing sunbath on the apartment lanai sounded like the best therapy. It would be a shame not to get a gorgeous tan while she had the chance. That thought was so pleasant that she drove past the Coronado nursery without stopping, and had to circle the block when she remembered the terra-cotta containers. She parked in front and went in to arrange for their planting. The shop had a large selection of palms to choose from, and the nurseryman agreed to have her order delivered in the next day or so.

Nicola went out to the curb with his young helper and left him unloading the heavy pieces from the station wagon while she returned to the showroom and completed the financial arrangements. At the last minute, she added a small glossy-leaved lemon tree to her order simply because she couldn't resist the fragrance of its blossoms.

Kevin Graham was emerging from the pool area when she came in the apartment-house lobby afterward. "Hey . . . let me help you with all that!" he insisted, hurrying to her side and taking the ceramic candelabrum and the witch piñata from her arms. "My lord," he went on as he surveyed the grim figure atop her broom, "where did you get this horror?"

"Old Town . . . this morning." Nicola hesitated as the elevator doors opened in front of them. "Really . . . you don't have to bother helping me. I can manage alone."

"Wouldn't think of it. Besides"—his attractive sunburned face creased in a grin—"I don't have much to do today, and keeping the clients happy is the most important part of my job." He jerked his head toward the open elevator. "I'll trail along."

He waited until they'd reached the upper floor and were walking down the hall before adding, "I hear you're on your own for a while. Our tenants' grapevine," he explained, "beats the CIA all hollow. It was a simple operation this time. Juliette's relaxing by the pool, and she reported Mr. Laird had gone on a fishing charter."

"I understand." Nicola unlocked the apartment door and gestured toward the living room. "Just put that piñata down anywhere. Mr. Laird sent me shopping with a prop list this morning . . ." She broke off as he gave her a quizzical look over his shoulder. "What's wrong?"

He looked slightly embarrassed as he placed the candelabrum and piñata on the davenport. "Nothing, really. It just seemed strange to hear you mention your husband so formally."

"Oh . . . that." She tried to keep her voice light as she covered her mistake. "I suppose it did sound a little silly. Out of business hours . . . things are different. I was his secretary before we were married, and I still do a lot of errands for the company like my trip to Old Town."

"That makes sense." He looked relieved and then puzzled as he picked up the witch piñata. "Damned if I can see why he'd want to take a picture of this."

"It *is* pretty ghastly, isn't it? Actually, I'm going to take that home as a souvenir. William might enjoy it." As Kevin looked expectant, she went on to explain. "He's a nice old gentleman who works for Alex."

"Sounds as if he has strange taste in women."

Nicola pictured William's reaction to that and had to hide a smile. "Well, each to his own. Thanks very much for bringing all this along."

Kevin lingered by the end table as if reluctant to leave. Absently he picked up the book she'd been reading the night before and flipped through the pages. "Mexican history, huh? This looks like an old-timer."

"I guess it is." Nicola watched him put it back. "It's one that was lent to Alex. I was reading it last night. There's some interesting detail on the monarchy if you like that era."

"Not my bag. Science fiction is my weakness, but don't let it get around." Kevin put his hands in his pockets and strolled with her toward the door. "Do you have any more fetching and carrying? I come pretty cheap." His tone was diffident, but he didn't hide the fact that he'd like to keep her company.

Two days before, Nicola would have made it easier by inviting him to stay for a cup of coffee. As it was, she simply smiled gratefully and shook her head. "There's nothing important left in the car. Alex can bring up the rest when he comes back—thanks all the same."

"My pleasure." He opened the hall door but lingered on the threshold. "I wonder why I meet all the interesting women after they've signed their lives away on a marriage license."

Nicola laughed. "Is *that* what I've done? Maybe I'd better write to my congressman and complain."

"You can joke about it, but it's the truth," Kevin groused. "I'm surprised you're not complaining already—being relegated to a fishing widow practically on your honeymoon."

Nicola wondered what he'd say if he knew the truth about her honeymoon, but decided that Juliette had probably covered that ground.

"I'd be happy to serve as a substitute in the meantime," Kevin was going on. "Just say the word, and I'm your man."

Nicola frowned, trying to catch up with the conversation. "What kind of a substitute are you talking about?"

"An escort to show you around town. I have tomorrow forenoon free . . ." He broke off and grinned. "What did you think I was offering?"

"I wasn't sure."

"That's what it sounded like." His grin

widened. "Naturally, I'd be glad to serve in any capacity. Just say the word, and I'll try and cancel a dinner date tonight."

"Don't be absurd. . . ."

"I'll be free by ten at the latest—even if I can't get out of it entirely. Afterward, I could pick you up and we could go dancing at a place I know in Mission Bay . . ." He broke off when she started to laugh. "What's the matter?"

She wiped her eyes with the edge of her hand. "Nothing—except I can see why you're in the real-estate business. What a salesman!"

"Never take 'no' for an answer—that's my motto. Did I make a sale this time?"

"Not for tonight, thanks. I've already made plans." She knew very well that Alex wouldn't subscribe to equal rights for fishing widows; not to the extent of finding consolation with another man.

"You're worried about your husband," Kevin said baldly. "Okay, I'll buy that. But what about tomorrow morning? He couldn't object to some innocent sightseeing. I'll even let you pick the places. How about it, Nicola?"

She was aware that he was shedding the last vestige of formality between them. On the other hand, there was certainly nothing wrong with a forenoon of sightseeing.

"I'd like that very much," she agreed finally. "What time shall I be ready?"

"If we start at nine, we can stop for coffee. I know a place . . ."

She laughed again. "I'm sure you do. Nine o'clock, then. I'll meet you in the lobby."

"Great, Nikki . . ." He started down the hall but pulled up after a step or two. "Oh, incidentally—my name's Kevin." He gave her a youthful grin. "See you tomorrow."

Nicola wore a thoughtful expression as she closed the apartment door after him and leaned against it. "Nikki" indeed! There was nothing youthful or inexperienced about the building manager's way with women. He must have cut his milk teeth learning to say all the right things.

She went into the kitchen and took two slices of bread from the drawer before searching in the refrigerator for a slice of cheese to put between them. She continued to think about her next day's sightseeing while she constructed a sandwich and poured a glass of milk to go with it. Then she took her lunch out onto the lanai and sat in the sunshine to eat it. Afterward she thought of changing and going down to the pool, but the prospect of an encounter with Juliette made her decide against it. She'd relax and enjoy the rest of the day by herself.

By the next morning, she was heartily sick of her enforced isolation. The silence had become oppressive after sundown the day before, and the evening had dragged interminably. She'd sampled all the television channels before switching the set off in frustration. Even the radio had more commercials than music, and eventually she'd turned that off, too. She drank a mug of soup standing by the sink and found herself wishing that Maria hadn't chosen to take Ivan the Terrible away. Even his yowls would have been preferable to the thick silence of the apartment.

She deliberately tried to keep her mind away from Alex, who was probably thoroughly enjoying his fishing trip, not pacing the floor and wondering what to do next. "Damn the man!" she had muttered, and moved restlessly back into the living room. She picked up the book on Maximilian and Carlota and then put it down again, beginning to understand why the Empress became a mental patient in her final years. Probably Maximilian went off on charter fishing trips, too! In which case, he'd deserved his fate.

It was just past nine o'clock when she gave up and put on her pajamas, only to lie tossing and turning as sleep evaded her. Finally she got up from the wide bed which harbored too many memories and took her pillow and blanket into the guest bedroom. The single bed had been stripped after Juliette's departure, but Nicola didn't bother to remake it. Instead, she simply curled up in a blanket atop the mattress and tried counting the sheep which had stubbornly eluded her in the other bedroom. Despite her best intentions, she found she was counting barracuda instead of woolly lambs, and the pasture fence had turned into a fish ladder before sleep finally claimed her.

The early night helped, though, and Nicola enjoyed her breakfast on the lanai the next morning, with sunlight dappling the floor and buttering the edges of the balcony railing.

Even after she'd washed her dishes and tidied the kitchen, there was time to do a quick housekeeping job on the other rooms. She changed the sheets in the master bedroom and then went on to make up the bed in the guestroom with fresh linen, as well. Once Alex returned, they could have a sensible discussion about future bedroom allotments. The phone rang while she was putting fresh towels in the bath, and she hurried to answer it.

When she picked up the receiver, she remembered that person who had called the day before and hesitated before putting it to her ear. Then she heard William's dignified tones coming across the long-distance wire from New York and sank down on the edge of the bed in relief.

Their conversation wasn't long, but tears of happiness came to Nicola's eyes when the old retainer gave his approval to her new position.

"But how did you hear so much about it?" she wanted to know.

"Mr. Alex, of course," William informed her. "He called yesterday to make sure that the painters would be through here in the house before you returned. They've promised to fin-

ish by the day after tomorrow, so everything
should work out very well. If you want anything special in decorating, you're to let me
know."

Nicola was too stunned to reply.

"Was there anything special you'd like done?"
William asked again.

"I . . . I don't think so. We haven't talked
about it." She thought fast. Evidently Alex
hadn't mentioned the temporary aspect of his
marriage—knowing that William certainly
wouldn't approve. "I'm sure everything will be
fine the way it is," she said eventually. "We'll
keep in touch."

She rang off after a few more minutes but
was still sitting on the edge of the bed when the
phone rang again. She picked up the receiver
thinking that William had called back with another message. "Did you forget something?" she
asked cheerily.

"I didn't," Kevin's voice replied. "I thought
you had. We did say nine o'clock, didn't we?"

Nicola looked at the bedroom clock and bit
her lip. "Oh, heavens, I'm sorry. I had no idea
that it was so late."

"That's all right . . . don't panic. I'm down
in the lobby whenever you're ready."

"Give me two minutes."

"I'll give you three. After that . . ."

"I'm on my way," she promised, and hung
up.

There was just time for an appraising glance

in the bedroom mirror to check her outfit of pink plaid pants and white sweater topped by a solid matching pink cardigan wrap which reached to her hips. Her oversized pouch bag of straw had hidden itself behind the mixer on the kitchen counter and took a little time to discover. After she'd retrieved it, Nicola stopped in the living room to stuff the book on Carlota into the top of it. Sometime during the morning, she'd transfer the book to the glove compartment of the station wagon. That way, she'd have it along when she eventually picked up Alex at the boat, and he could give it to the fishing captain as he'd promised.

Kevin was blowing some dust from one of the lobby philodendrons when she emerged from the elevator.

"I'm terribly sorry," she apologized. "Everything took longer than I thought. At the last minute, I couldn't find my purse."

He gave the big shoulder bag an amused appraisal and shook his head. "I'll never understand women. How do you lose something that size? It could double as a picnic basket on weekends."

She grinned companionably and fell into step beside him as he started for the lobby doors. "It's doubled as a lunch box more times than I can count. That way I don't need a brown bag. Not only that, I can carry Alex's sunglasses and extra film—all the things men can't get into their pockets these days." Her sideways glance was teasing. "Don't you have a jacket or something that needs packing?"

"This is southern California—who needs jackets? Although," he admitted with a quick look at the sky, "I think I should have put on a long-sleeved shirt. It's a little drafty today when you get in the shade."

"And here I was admiring your wardrobe selection," she told him in a professional tone. His rust-and-black geometric-print shirt looked expensive and blended perfectly with his rust gabardine slacks. Until he led the way to a compact car parked nearby, she was deciding that her first impression of the man was wrong; he was showing more sophisticated tastes than she had imagined. As she waited for him to unlock the door, she said, "You have me puzzled."

"I'm glad to hear it. That means I've made some kind of impression." He swung the car door open and waited for her to get in.

When he had settled into the driver's seat, she went on. "Seriously, I would have said that a sports car was more your style. Am I right?"

His answering grin was frank. "When you sell apartments, it isn't good business to drive a more expensive car than your clients'. The only reason I'm telling you this is that you're a stranger on the scene. I can trust you not to give away my trade secrets, can't I?"

She raised her palm solemnly. "Hope to die." Then her lips curved. "I'm betting you sell a lot of apartments. Especially to women."

"I refuse to answer that. . . ."

Her smile widened. "On the grounds that you might incriminate yourself?"

There was nothing of the undergraduate in his answering glance. "It doesn't do to be too honest. Take you, for instance . . ." Before she could interrupt, he added softly, "And don't think that hasn't occurred to me."

"It's a little early in the day for that kind of talk," she managed after an instant's confusion. "You caught me off guard."

"Does it bother you?"

"Not especially." She matched his cool tone. "I've heard that theme used before—usually when bachelors are talking to married women who aren't a threat to their freedom. Aren't you afraid one of your prospects might take you seriously?"

"That's what I keep hoping for. Besides," he reproved, "there aren't that many."

Nicola broke out laughing. "I don't believe a word of it. Not when all you have to do is say the word and a gorgeous creature like Juliette comes running." She turned in the seat to watch his profile. "It was obvious that you were old friends."

"So old that the bloom is gone." He shrugged. "Oh, Juliette's okay—a little intense for steady dating, but her job keeps her so busy that she's not on the West Coast often. As your husband knows." His glance met hers for an instant before he concentrated on the bridge traffic. "I understand that they're old friends, too."

"They've worked together for several years. Alex says that she's unbeatable for his high-fashion accounts." Nicola kept her tone casual, determined not to let him know that his comment had hurt. Alex had never discussed his personal relationship with Juliette in past months other than to ask Nicola to order flowers for her birthday or make dinner reservations when he was too busy to take care of such details. It had given her a twinge of pain even in those days; now she was surprised at her intense reaction.

She turned to look at the passing landscape, and changed the subject. "Where are we bound for?"

"How about a trip to the zoo for starters? This afternoon, we can drive out to the Mission San Diego on the edge of town." He was turning toward the Cabrillo freeway even as he spoke. "The zoo's apt to be crowded later, but at this hour we don't have to worry."

"It sounds wonderful," she agreed, glad that they were on impersonal ground again. "I've heard about this zoo for years."

"It's one of the best in the world," he confirmed, watching a passing car. "Too bad that we don't have time to visit their wild-animal park north of town. It's developed on a big scale and patterned after the African game reserves. Be sure and see it before you leave."

"I'll try. Right now, I'm looking forward to viewing that new shipment of koala bears from Australia I've been reading about. They're supposed to be in a special exhibit." She turned toward him impulsively. "This is awfully nice of you. It's much more fun for me than going alone."

"Don't gild the lily too much. You were right about bachelors having ulterior motives. Especially with brides whose husbands schedule out-of-town fishing trips to Baja."

"How did you know where he was going?"

"Beats me—maybe I heard it from Juliette. Anyhow, it doesn't take much imagination. Most of the charter boats from here go to the Coronado Islands or Baja on their overnight trips. If you're just out for the day, you usually end up off La Jolla."

"I see," she murmured. "I didn't know it was so cut-and-dried."

"Actually, it depends on how the fish are running." Kevin slowed the car and turned into one of the zoo's huge parking lots as he spoke. "That husband of yours isn't apt to have much luck. These days the seals wait in line for a man to hook a fish, and then swipe everything but the head."

"I don't imagine it matters much to the fish."

"The end result is the same," he agreed. "It doesn't improve a fisherman's temper, though."

"You sound as if you've been that route."

"Guilty as charged. I've come back empty-handed too many times." He pulled up in a parking space and turned off the ignition. As he got out to open her door, he added, "Fishing is just one vice of mine. You'll find out about the others as we go along."

She managed to keep a solemn expression. "I'm not sure whether that's a threat or a promise. However, since yours is the best offer I've had this morning . . ."

"And the only one."

"And the only one," she confirmed, "I'll keep it in mind. But first, the koala bears, and after that, a cup of coffee."

"You're giving me a hard act to follow," he grumbled, taking her arm and heading toward the main gate. "Like that adage about 'virtue being its own punishment.'"

"That's the whole idea," she told him, laughing. "Don't worry, the practice will be good for you."

Later, she had to admit that his manners couldn't be faulted. He—was an attentive, amusing escort as they wandered through the children's zoo, and he waited while Nicola stared at the members of the koala colony, who munched on their eucalyptus leaves, unaware that they were Australia's special gift and the superstars of the zoo.

When Kevin boosted Nicola onto a zoo bus for a leisurely motor tour of the rest of the exhibits, he obligingly took over a cameraman's duties while she ogled the animals displayed along the route,

"I thought we were going to lose you in that last bear moat," he complained to her as they headed for a cup of coffee at a refreshment stand near the entrance when the tour was finished. "You didn't tell me that you were an animal nut."

"I was laughing at their names. Somebody has a wonderful sense of humor around here—imagine calling those cubs 'Raz-bear' and 'Boysen-bear.' "

"Maybe it was the same person who named the koalas 'Cough Drop,' 'Pepsi,' and 'Coke.' "

"Don't forget the other two, 'Waltzing' and 'Matilda.' " She shook her head in wonderment. "And what a life—just eat and sleep!"

"The sleeping's okay, but a diet of eucalyptus leaves 365 days a year wouldn't thrill me." He got in line at the refreshment counter. "Speaking of food—would you like something with your coffee?"

"Just a place to sit down—if that's all right."

"One park bench coming up," he promised solemnly, "along with the coffee."

Nicola waited while he paid for the coffee and then took her Styrofoam container before walking with him to a wooden bench near a border of irislike plants. She reached out to touch a leaf and said idly, "I read somewhere that the zoo's botanical collection is even more fabulous than the animals. Just imagine—all this and sunshine, too! I wonder if San Diego people know how lucky they are."

Kevin was surveying her thoughtfully. "I never thought about it. It's nice to know that enthusiasm hasn't gone out of style."

"Don't underestimate the charm of a koala bear," she said with a smile. "It's a change for me to see something that isn't artificial. In our business, most of the people have a surface gloss that can wear thin in a hurry."

"Your husband excepted, of course."

"Of course!" Nicola said emphatically. "Whatever his other faults, Alex is as honest as they come."

"Very commendable. He's a hard dog to keep under the porch."

Nicola almost choked on a swallow of coffee. "I'm sorry," she said, recovering. "I didn't know we were trying."

"You can't blame me." Kevin finished his coffee and reached over to shove the empty container in a litter can. "I suppose that Juliette doesn't rate as high in your estimation."

"I hardly know her—except in a business way." Nicola stood up and disposed of her Styrofoam mug as well. "I'd like to have a profile and measurements like hers. She makes me feel like Boysen-bear when I get in the same room with her. Especially around the waistline."

Kevin's somber air deserted him as he laughed and gave Nicola an impulsive hug. "If I ever saw a woman who didn't have to worry about measurements . . ." He shook his head. "I'd better stop right there. That husband of yours is bigger than I am."

"Worse still, he might decide to break the lease. That's what you're really worried about." As they started strolling toward the main gate, she added, "Don't worry. I won't let him. Not after you've been so nice to me today."

"Hey—we're not finished yet. There's still time for the mission, isn't there?"

She checked a zoo clock near the exit. "I think so. If it doesn't take too long. After that, I'd better get back to the apartment. I don't know what time Alex is coming back."

His eyes went toward the heavens. "There's that name again. I suppose that's one of the penalties of going out with a married woman."

"Only one? Now I'm curious—what are the others?"

"I'll let you know later," he said obliquely, "provided the right opportunity presents itself."

Nicola wondered what he meant, and then forgot about it until later, when they had driven to the famous Mission San Diego. They were fortunate in finding the historic spot almost deserted, and strolled through the grounds in leisurely fashion. The undersized old chambers of the mission were kept in such excellent shape that it was hard to believe the adobe walls and arches dated back to 1769, when Father Junípero Serra had founded the California mission chain. Warm earth tones predominated in the Spartan furnishings of the priest's room, with beige and brown Indian blankets on the rough floor and atop the rawhide-laced bed. The rich brown shades merged to sienna and gold on the beautiful altar in the mission church, but a primitive air prevailed even there, with the quarry tiles on the floor showing the wear of generations of worshipers.

When Nicola finally followed Kevin out into the old cemetery-garden behind the bell wall of the mission, she gasped with surprise and pleasure. The vividness of the flowerbeds was almost unbelievable; bougainvillea and lush shrubbery competed for attention with palm trees bordered by geraniums and marguerites. A hedge of Natal plum next to a waist-high wall beside Nicola added a magnificent fragrance to the air.

"It's perfectly lovely!" Nicola's hands went out in an inarticulate gesture. "And so quiet and peaceful. We must be the only people around. I'm so glad you suggested coming here."

He stared down at her for a moment without replying. Then he said, "I had an ulterior motive. If you'll remember . . ."—his fingers lifted her chin gently but firmly—"I even warned you." The last words came out softly as he bent down and kissed her.

Taken completely by surprise, Nicola remained motionless in his embrace until he finally raised his head. His expression was hard to fathom as he met her glance. "Maybe if we tried again, we might do better," he drawled, and reached out to draw her closer.

She sidestepped and shook her head. "No."

"That's all you can say—just no."

She smiled slightly. "Would it sound better if I said, 'No, thank you'?"

"You don't look like the kind of woman who'd let a marriage license make that much difference," he said, stepping back and letting his hand drop.

"Appearances can be deceiving," she told him frankly. "You aren't the only one who's surprised. Let's walk through the rest of the garden, shall we?" She moved on down the path and felt him fall into step beside her after she'd gone a little way. Thank heaven he wasn't going to argue about her lack of response to his overtures.

She was surprised herself that she'd felt nothing during that embrace. Alex's kiss on the dock had left her reeling, but her pulse rate had scarcely accelerated in Kevin's arms. She frowned as she thought about it. Kevin was tall and nice-looking—better-looking than Alex, to be strictly honest. But there was more to it than a profile. . . .

Kevin was watching the way her features mirrored her thoughts. "There are exceptions to every rule," he commented after noting her puzzled frown. "No reason that you have to stop breathing and enjoying some of the good things in life merely because you have a husband. Even your pal Maximilian had more than affairs of state going when he was in Mexico."

A wry smile crossed Nicola's features. "Maybe that's what finally drove Carlota to a padded room."

"She might have been in better shape if she'd chosen the same kind of therapy as her husband," Kevin said flatly.

"I'll remember that if Alex plans another fishing trip while we're here," Nicola replied in the same tone, "but I'm afraid that just one overnight charter doesn't entitle me to toss my bonnet over the windmill."

A dull red crept up under his cheekbones. "Sorry . . . I seem to have said the wrong thing."

"Not really." She swung around to face him as they reached the exit. "You've improved my morale a hundred percent, which I suspect you knew all along. How many other fishing widows live in that apartment house?"

"If you think I'm going to answer that, you're crazy," he said, sounding more like the likable, uncomplicated man she'd thought him in the first place. He took her elbow companionably as they started toward the mission parking lot. "I know of a place on the waterfront that serves terrific seafood," he went on when they reached the car. "People come down from Los Angeles to try the abalone."

"It sounds like fun, but I have to get back to the apartment."

"Oh, I didn't mean for lunch," he assured her as he turned the ignition key and started the motor. "As a matter of fact, this place doesn't open until dinner. There's no point in your sitting around all evening if Alex hasn't returned."

"Can't do it. I've already made other plans . . . worse luck." She crossed her fingers under the edge of her slacks as she spoke. It was understandable how Kevin might have gotten the wrong idea a few minutes before in the mission garden, but she was taking no more chances. Once was an honest mistake—twice could become a habit.

"Maybe another time," Kevin said easily as he pulled onto the arterial fronting the mission property. "Juliette says you'll be here awhile, and we might as well take advantage of your spare time."

Nicola merely nodded noncommittally, wondering if Alex really had discussed his future plans with the model. He certainly hadn't been any fund of information with his wife.

She was still smarting under that bald truth when Kevin drove up in front of their Coronado apartment building a little later. "Here we are, home sweet home . . . and no one the wiser," he said.

"If I'd known we were doing something shady, you could have delivered me to the back door in a laundry hamper," she commented wryly.

"We don't have a back door here. Only the magnificent Pacific on one side and spellbinding Glorietta Bay on the other." He leaned across her to open the car door on her side.

"That sounds suspiciously like a real-estate pamphlet," she said, getting out and leaning down to thank him.

"Page one, paragraph one of our sales brochure," he admitted. "Now I can put you on my expense account for the morning."

"To think I was worried about you. At this rate, you'll be running for governor in five years—and winning."

He grinned back at her, unabashed. "I'm just following your rules. If you change your mind about dinner . . ."

"I'll make an appointment." She closed the door and returned his wave as he drove off.

Nicola had started for the lobby before she remembered the book in her tote bag. She retraced her way to the parking lot, unlocked the station wagon, and stored the history book in the glove compartment under the dashboard. As she straightened, she caught a glimpse of Pat Towne's cargo, which was still in the back. She'd have to dispose of it before she could fit Alex and his belongings into the car on his return.

She glanced at her watch and then went around to slip behind the wheel of the station wagon. There wasn't a chance of Alex returning so early in the day—so what better time to drive back to the dock and see if she could find permanent storage for Pat's belongings.

The drive back across the bridge toward the sport-fishing piers was uneventful; by then she was familiar enough with the freeway that she was able to make her way easily to the Harbor Drive exit. The waters of San Diego Bay on her left looked placid and inviting in the sunlight. Probably the skippers of the sailing dinghies off Harbor Island were disgruntled with the lack of breeze, but the cyclists and joggers on the shore highway appeared to be enjoying it.

Nicola drove automatically, wondering if Alex was experiencing the same good weather off the coast. If the fish were biting, he'd probably be oblivious of a full-fledged hurricane. Her expression became thoughtful. It might be fun to go on a fishing trip and see what was so fascinating. She might even become so expert that Alex would be impressed and insist on her company the next time.

Then she shook her head in disgust, knowing there wasn't any future to such thinking. If Alex had wanted her along, he merely had to mention it. Which he hadn't.

If more women faced facts, they wouldn't be disillusioned in the first place, Nicola told herself fiercely as she parked next to the charterboat marina. The decision made her march firmly into the waterfront office. She might not know how to bait a hook, but she did know how to clean out the back of a station wagon.

Her arguments were so persuasive that the marina manager took personal charge of the removal of Pat's cargo and apologized for the inconvenience to Nicola.

"It's all my fault," he said, reaching into the car and piling the Mexican blankets in a cardboard carton. "I should have been around to take care of this stuff in the first place. Pat will take my head off when he hears what happened. He's paid for a storage locker just for stuff like this. Lots of times his charter passengers have to arrange shipment of their Mexican purchases back home." The manager hauled out a painted ceramic container and packed it between the blankets. "I'm sure sorry that you had to make an extra trip," he went on, discovering that Nicola's attention was on the deserted pier next to the marina. "I don't imagine most of the boats will be back until late . . . I've heard that the fishing's pretty good out there." He saw the sudden slump of her shoulders and said sympathetically, "Married to an eager one, huh? You should have gone along."

"I wasn't asked. I know one end of a fishing rod from the other, but that's as far as I go. Does anybody around here take out beginners?" she asked.

The marina manager scratched his thinning hair. "I hire out my boat once in a while."

"For a half-day trip? Maybe off La Jolla," she urged, remembering. "I'm not sure how well I'd do out on the ocean."

"Offshore's about as far as you can go on a half-day trip and still get any fishing in. I have some time off tomorrow afternoon—how would that be?"

Nicola surveyed his stocky figure and pleasant ordinary face. "Tomorrow afternoon will be fine," she said, making a sudden decision. "Do I come here?"

He shook his head. "My boat's berthed at Mission Bay. I live out that way, and it's more convenient. I'll draw you a map how to get to the marina there." He reached in his shirt pocket as he spoke and drew out a small notebook to sketch the directions. "You won't have any trouble," he said, handing the map to her a minute later. "I'll be on the lookout for you at the marina by Quivira Basin around noon tomorrow."

"What do I bring?" Nicola asked as she tucked his sketch carefully in her purse.

"I'll take care of the tackle if you'll take care of the lunch. That's my usual arrangement."

She gave a pleased nod. "That's easy. Do you think I can really catch something? Something big enough to take home?"

He chuckled at her enthusiasm. "I sure as hell hope so. I plan on doing some fishing myself, and I haven't come back empty-handed yet.

Remember, though—we'll probably just be going for bottom fish."

Nicola didn't have the slightest notion what he meant by that. "The only kind of sport fish I've heard about are marlin and swordfish."

He looked shaken. "I can tell you, lady—there aren't any of those on the bottom here. You've been reading the wrong books. Did your husband claim he was going for that kind of catch?"

"Oh, no," she said hastily. "I warned you that I didn't know anything about it. The only reason I want to charter a boat is so I can land something on a hook by myself."

"For a minute there, you had me worried," he said, stepping back as she got in the station wagon. "We can come back with some kind of catch. Even if we strike out, there's always the fish market on the way home."

"Probably I'd be smarter if I started at the fish market, but I'll try it the hard way. Noon tomorrow, then—see you."

The prospect of the outing improved her spirits so much that she detoured by the airport coffee shop on the drive back and bought a hamburger to take out. Minutes later, she parked by the maritime museum and ate her lunch in the car watching the colorful waterfront activity. Alex wasn't going to be the only one enjoying his vacation, she decided. If he needed somebody to run his errands in town tomorrow afternoon, he could recruit Juliette.

There was a note in the apartment mailbox when she returned, stating that Maria would not be back to work for a few more days. At the bottom of the letter, however, there was an almost indecipherable postscript which said that the cat might be coming sooner.

"So poor Ivan's getting the boot," Nicola murmured to herself as she rode up in the elevator. "Either he misses his oatmeal, or Maria misses her sleep."

The apartment living room looked like an attractive refuge when Nicola let herself in. She made a casual tour of the rest of the rooms to see if any of the apartment staff had delivered a note from Alex saying when he planned to return, but all the tabletops were bare. Evidently he was going to be content to call her when they docked rather than communicate by ship-to-shore channels.

Nicola wandered back through the living room and went out on the sunlit lanai. She sank in a canvas lounger for a few minutes and then decided that her role as a lady of leisure wasn't especially appealing.

At that moment the telephone rang, and she scrambled back to the living room, trying not to sound breathless as she answered. Unfortunately, it wasn't the call she had hoped for; the neighborhood nursery had finished the planting she'd ordered and wanted to know if they could deliver the containers the next day.

Nicola stifled a sigh and agreed to a morning

delivery. After hanging up, she made no pretense of going back to the lanai, but decided on a relaxing bath instead.

Afterward she searched the freezer to find something for dinner. The noodle casserole she chose wasn't exciting, but neither was the television movie which she selected to accompany it. When a news program followed, she reached over to turn off the set.

She wandered into the guest bedroom just as the clock chimed ten, and five minutes later she was in bed with the lights off. As she stretched out between the chilly sheets and stared at the ceiling, she decided that her honeymoon had probably established a new low for the book of records.

It didn't come as any great surprise to find that insomnia was another problem on her lengthening list. When she thought about it dispassionately—and she had plenty of time— sleeplessness followed right along in logical progression.

A half-hour later, another item was added to the agenda when she discovered that her stomach and Ivan's shared the same "demand-feeding" schedule. By then, her frozen dinner was merely a memory, and absolute starvation loomed larger and larger in her mind.

Deciding not to fight it any longer, she pushed back the covers and turned on the bed-lamp. Hot milk might help, she reasoned as she reached for her robe. A handful of cookies had

been added to the menu by the time she found
her slippers and padded up the hallway. There
was enough light sifting through the half-open
door of the bedroom behind her that she didn't
bother to switch on any other illumination.
When she reached the kitchen, she merely
flicked on the tiny spotlight in the hood over
the stove before getting milk from the refrigerator and finding a small saucepan in the cupboard.

She stared through the kitchen window down
toward the dark expanse of Glorietta Bay while
the milk was heating. A thin cloud layer partially obscured the moon and the landing lights
of a navy plane which was descending on its final approach. The jet noise receded as the aircraft passed out of sight, and Nicola became
conscious of another sound—the hissing of milk
as it boiled up to the top of the saucepan.

She darted back to the stove and yanked the
pot off the burner. For a minute she considered
pouring the scalding milk down the drain.
Then she took the easy way out and poured it
instead into the mug she had waiting on the
counter. The saucepan was filled with water
and left to soak in the sink until morning.

Nicola switched off the stove light and picked
up the mug to take it into the bedroom, when
she heard a faint noise from the hallway.

She froze in her tracks, stopping so abruptly
that some milk splashed unnoticed onto the linoleum by her slippered feet.

There was an interval of silence as she remained in the kitchen doorway. When she'd just started to relax her death grip on the handle of the mug, there came the metallic sound of a key being inserted in the lock, and, an instant later, the noise of the bolt being turned.

Nicola moved out into the shadowed dining room as the hall door opened and a tall, dark figure came stealthily into the foyer. She could see his outline as he carefully edged the door shut behind him and stayed crouched beside it, making sure that his entrance had gone unnoticed.

By then Nicola's heart sounded like a piledriver in her ears. The thumping was so loud that she was surprised it couldn't be heard across the expanse of slate floor between them. Belatedly she realized that she should have escaped down the back service stairs the minute he'd opened the front door. That way, she could have fled to the lobby and gotten help from the security men on duty.

Now it was too late for anything except a confrontation—and then trying to escape in the confusion.

Once she made the decision, she put her plan in action. Her hand switched on the overhead light, and an instant later she was plunging straight toward the door. As she came abreast of the man, she let fly with the hot milk.

Nicola's aim was deplorable, but the shock

value was unsurpassed—possibly because she identified him as she completed the delivery.

Alex had only that split second to see a robed creature swooping toward him before he was showered with a sheet of steaming white liquid.

He lurched backward, forgetting about his bad ankle, which gave way on the waxed slate floor.

A second later he hit that same slate floor with a thud that made Nicola wince and close her eyes.

When she opened them, she saw Alex stretched motionless at her feet, with hot milk still dripping from his hair.

7

"Oh, dear God!" The words came out in a whimper when she knelt at Alex's side, searching frantically for a pulse and finally finding it. His face was ashen and his eyes remained closed as she timed the reassuringly regular beat. For additional comfort she put her ear against his chest and listened to the rhythm again until she got dizzy and realized she was holding her own breath.

She sat up then and tried massaging his hands to revive him. "Alex . . . can you hear me? Please open your eyes and tell me you're all right," she begged in a fervent whisper. When there was no response, she mopped the tears from her face and tried to think. Would cold water bring him around, or should she phone for emergency help?

Her glance lingered on his chest, and its regular movement made her decide that it wouldn't hurt to get some water and try once more to revive him. She struggled to her feet and cast a last anxious look at his still figure before hurrying toward the kitchen.

She snatched a clean towel from the drawer and ran water over it until it was dripping. Then she sped back through the dining room with it, ignoring the faint trail of water she was leaving behind.

Alex was still in the same position as before. Nicola made an unhappy murmur as she went down on her knees beside him, draping the towel over his forehead. A moment later she was stricken to see a new trickle of liquid running down his ear—only, this time it was cold water instead of hot milk.

It was also enough to make Alex's eyes flutter open. "Dammit to hell . . ." he complained, trying to move out of reach. "You don't have to drown me now because you missed scalding me on the first go-round."

"You're all right, after all," Nicola managed to say. "You could have told me . . ."

Alex's recoil wasn't entirely due to the lump on his head. "My God, if that isn't just like a woman. Scare a man to death and then wonder why he doesn't leap up off the tiles and apologize for living."

She corrected him automatically. "That's slate, not tile."

"Believe me, I'm not apt to forget. Their texture has been embedded in my memory forever." He sat up and cautiously felt his skull.

"As well as permanently embedded in the back of my head."

"I'm terribly sorry about that. . . ." She felt some water on her instep and looked down to see that she was still clutching the sopping towel. "I think you should have this . . ."

"Not on your Nellie! My ear's still full of milk from your first try." He squinted up at her painfully. "Who in the hell were you expecting?"

"I wasn't expecting anybody. That's the whole point." Nicola found it hard to be dignified with a slipper full of water. "I certainly didn't think you'd come sneaking in at this time of night."

"Next time I'll hire a brass band to lead the way." He got to his feet with an effort. "Could we have the rest of this discussion someplace where there's a little padding?"

Nicola ignored his sarcasm; she was far more disturbed by the way he swayed as he tried to stay erect, and the pallor of his skin. "Hang on to me," she commanded.

"Get rid of that crying towel first."

She looked around for a suitable place and finally just dropped it on the slate by the door before putting an arm around his waist. "Can you make it to the bedroom?" she wanted to know.

"I guess so. I'd planned on a detour by the kitchen."

"Honestly, Alex—you're the limit!" she burst

out, letting annoyance hide her relief. "Probably you have a concussion, and all you can think about is food."

"That's not the only thing," he said, letting her lead him down the hallway toward the bedroom, "but right now it's the safest thing. That tidal wave you launched took five years off my life."

"I *said* I was sorry," she said, wishing she could sink through the floor. "I didn't dream it was you. I thought it was the sneak thief who went through our bags, or that man who scared me on the telephone."

"That's the trouble with you," Alex complained as they reached the master bedroom and he sank on the edge of the mattress. "The only exercise you get these days is leaping to conclusions."

"Well, you could have let me know you were coming," she said, standing uncertainly beside him.

"I did try late this afternoon." He raked a hand through his damp hair. "There wasn't any answer."

Nicola felt a surge of compassion. "I was out. . . ." Then, before he could probe further, she changed the subject. "You'd better see a doctor right away. Should I call the one they advised for your ankle?"

"He probably doesn't handle the other end of patients." Alex's chin took a stubborn tilt. "Besides, there's no need to call anybody. As soon as I gather some strength, I'll go in and clean up. I can't see why Cleopatra recommended milk baths—they're sticky as hell."

Nicola ignored that and said sharply, "You're certainly not going to move around in a tile bathroom. Don't be an idiot!"

He took a deep breath. "You're in no position to cast stones. Talk about pestilential nuisances . . ." He broke off as if getting a grip on himself, and then stood up. "I'm also going to take off these clothes—the odor of fish bait and hot milk is getting to me."

"Stay right there," Nicola cautioned him as she moved to the closet. "I'll find your pajamas. After you've changed, you can see how you feel. Please, Alex," she begged as she reappeared, "just for me. You've had an awful crack on the head."

He took the pajamas and put them on the mattress beside him as he gave her an amused look. "Do you think I can be trusted to undress alone? There's always a chance that I could keel over."

Nicola flushed, but she returned his glance squarely. "In that case, be sure and fall toward the bed so the doctor will know where to find you. I'll go put the teakettle on."

"Discreet . . . oh, so discreet."

She had a good idea what he murmured, but she brazened it out. "I beg your pardon?"

"Never mind. You wouldn't like it." He finished unbuttoning his shirt and tossed it toward a chair in the corner.

As she watched his hands go toward his cotton slacks, she said hurriedly, "Now you're being childish. I may have to call the doctor, after all."

He jerked the belt out of his pants and threw it in the same direction as the shirt. "You do, my girl, and you'll be sorry. I mean it." He didn't raise his voice, but his tone made Nicola bite her lip and leave the room abruptly.

All the time she was heating the teakettle in the kitchen, she wondered whether to call his bluff. It would afford her tremendous satisfaction to be able to go back and announce that the doctor was on his way. She'd have trouble justifying her actions, though, since Alex wasn't showing any suspicious symptoms. On the contrary, he was thinking all too clearly. He had just shown what he thought of a wife who bolted from the bedroom as soon as he bared his chest. If she'd had any sense, she would have offered to help him undress and forced *him* to seek refuge.

That theory was so absurd, she knew Alex would have roared with laughter at the idea. If ever there was a man who didn't need tutoring on human anatomy, he was the one. Especially after winning a national award for photographing some Scandinavian beauties the year before. Suddenly Nicola felt like a sandlot player pinch-hitting in the World Series, knowing all she'd done so far in the contest was strike out—resoundingly.

She poured boiling water into a teapot and let it steep while she put two mugs on a tray. After looking at her watch, she decided it was safe to go back. This time she'd act like a modern, rational-thinking woman who wouldn't go skulking into the shrubbery every time a four-letter word came into the conversation.

"You look as if you've been up to something," Alex greeted her when she arrived back at the bedroom holding the tray carefully in front of her.

"You're imagining things—I was just making your tea," she replied calmly, glad to see that he had gotten into bed after donning his pajamas. The pajama top was evidently an afterthought, because he hadn't bothered to button it. Nicola dragged her glance away from his broad expanse of chest and concentrated on putting the tray down without an accident.

"No telephone calls?" He was watching her closely.

She shook her head. "I decided there was no point in raising your blood pressure along with everything else. This hot, sweet tea is supposed to be good for shock."

"In that case, you'd better drink yours, too." He leaned over to get his mug. "I found an ice bag in the bathroom. That should complete the cure."

Her lips tightened at the way he'd ignored her warnings about walking around.

He was quick to notice it. "It's all right. I moved like a turtle and hung on all the way. It felt good to finally find some soap and hot water. The heater on the boat wasn't working properly, so Pat and I were reeking of fish at the end."

"How did the trip go, otherwise?" Nicola kept her attention on her mug of tea.

"I didn't have any luck in Ensenada, if that's what you mean. Either the word's out about the police, or all the merchandise has been moved to market. For lord's sake, why don't you sit down instead of hovering?" He frowned and gestured toward the end of the bed. "You'll be safe down there. I've given up making any more sudden moves tonight."

"I'm not worried about that," she explained, doing as he asked. "I just thought you should keep as quiet as possible. Since you won't let me call the doctor."

"That's still bothering you, isn't it?"

She rubbed her finger around the top of her mug. "You were a little brutal about it."

His eyebrows went up. "The only thing that's suffered is your pride. You know damned well that you'd have called the doctor if you'd thought it was necessary—even if you had to lock me in here."

Her lips twitched. "Just so you realize it."

He stared steadily back at her. "Don't

worry—I've never underestimated you. I've made some other mistakes, maybe, but not that. Of course, you've made a few, too."

"It's a good thing I didn't call the doctor; you're getting back to normal in a hurry. Here—I'll take that." She reached over to put his empty mug on the tray, and placed hers beside it. "Where did you say that ice bag was?"

"On the hamper in the bathroom." He watched her move gracefully across the room to get it, noting the attractive lines of her figure under the thin nylon-jersey robe. His expression was carefully noncommittal as she came back by the bed again and put the ice bag on the tray.

"I'll fill it in the kitchen." She glanced worriedly down at him. "Do you think you'll be able to sleep then?"

"If I take a couple of aspirin." He pushed back the covers to get out of bed, when she stopped him with a fierce gesture.

"I'll bring you some. *Will* you stay put?"

He subsided with a sigh. "There's not much else I can do. Lord, it's quiet in this place. I can see why Ivan objected to being deserted."

Nicola wanted to confess that she hadn't cared much for her lonely sojourn either. She contented herself with saying, "Maria left a note that Ivan may be back tomorrow. I got the feeling he's in disgrace, so he's being sent to Siberia. That's us," she added ungrammatically.

Alex looked pleased at the news. "I hope

Juliette's aunt doesn't mind if he sharpens his teeth on her furniture. Unfortunately, you'll have to chaperon him during the photograph session. I thought I'd start working around noon."

Nicola opened her mouth to argue, but a quick look showed that Alex wasn't in any condition for long conversations. She picked up the tray and walked toward the door. "I'll be right back with the ice bag and the aspirin."

Alex watched her go with a faint scowl, aware of her sudden hesitation but puzzled as to the reason. Clearly his lovely, stubborn Nicola was playing a game of her own, but just then he was too weary to figure it out.

The aspirin should help. So would some sleep. That had been in short supply aboard the boat . . . along with the fish. Pat Towne hadn't been forthcoming, either. All in all, the trip was a complete write-off as far as finding out anything for Marco Alvarez and his men. Tomorrow he'd have to call and tell him so. Alex's scowl deepened as he thought of that.

Nicola caught the tail end of his expression when she came back into the room. "Are you feeling worse?"

The telephone rang shrilly before he could answer.

"I'll get it," she said, handing him the aspirin and a glass of water while she reached for the phone. "Hello?"

There was a short pause at the other end,

and then a masculine voice said, "Mr. Laird, please."

"Just a moment." She cupped her hand over the mouthpiece to ask Alex, "Do you want to take it?"

"Animal or vegetable?"

"Male animal. Sounds pretty dishy."

"You're a big help." He reached for the receiver. "This is Laird. Oh . . . yeah . . . just a minute." Alex turned his head toward Nicola. "Were you going to get that ice bag?"

Nicola's cheeks flooded with color. "Of course. It's still in the kitchen. I'll wrestle with the ice cubes." She closed the bedroom door carefully behind her.

It didn't take a magic ball to see that Alex wanted her out of the room, but she resented his attempt to gloss it over. All he had to say was, "This is private," and she would have understood. Certainly he'd done it in the past. Then she realized that secretaries didn't have any right to question mysterious phone calls, but wives fortunately were in a different category.

As soon as she'd filled the ice bag, she decided to put her theory to the test.

Alex was still on the phone when she returned to the bedroom, but he didn't prolong the conversation. He merely said, "All right, then. We'll talk about it tomorrow after I've asked some questions. I'll call you." Then he leaned over and replaced the receiver.

Nicola stood by the bureau, shifting the ice bag from one hand to the other. When he stared quizzically at her, she said, "I'll put something around this so it won't drip," and detoured to the linen closet in the bathroom. After wrapping the rubberized bag in a thin terry towel, she went back to the side of the bed and handed it to him. "You look terrible," she said frankly when she'd made a closer inspection of his drawn features. "I don't think the aspirin helped. You shouldn't have taken that phone call—even if it was a friend of yours. . . ."

She let her voice trail off suggestively, but Alex merely grunted, flinching as he tried to adjust the ice bag on his head.

"It was a friend, wasn't it?" Nicola persisted.

Alex said something that sounded like "Umph" and closed his eyes.

Nicola's lips tightened as she stared down at his recumbent form. So much for conjugal rights! She waited a minute longer and then stalked toward the bedroom door, the hem of her robe making angry swishing sounds around her ankles. Alex's voice caught her on the threshold.

"Where in the devil do you think you're going?"

She whirled to face him, noticing that he hadn't moved except for opening his eyes in the interval. "I'm going to bed—obviously."

"There's nothing obvious about it," he retorted. "Which bed? Or are we playing twenty questions again?" He heaved a sigh which was audible all the way across the room. "I'm not in the mood to play games tonight."

"That was the farthest thing from my mind. I've already been to bed earlier in the guest room." She tried to sound polite and reasonable. "This was the arrangement we agreed on."

"Before this last escapade," he pointed out. "Frankly, I feel like hell. It would be nice to have you a little nearer for the next few hours in case I need anything. If you don't mind."

When he spoke like that, Nicola felt like Lucrezia Borgia readying her poison ring. "I'm sorry—I didn't realize . . ." she stammered in confusion. "Maybe I'd better call the doctor, after all."

"That isn't necessary. Everything will probably be okay, but I don't want to take any chances." He yanked on the edge of the sheet, trying to get comfortable, and succeeded in making a shambles of the bedclothes.

"Here, let me straighten that for you." Nicola went over to fix the blanket and then arrange his pillow when he struggled with that.

"I'll try not to disturb you," he promised, putting the ice bag on his forehead as he sat up.

"That ice won't do any good there," Nicola told him in some exasperation. "For heaven's sake, put it where the bump is."

"I was hot . . ."

"That's better than getting chilled." She

straightened to give him a worried look. "I'll come back after I get my pillow—if that's what you want."

"Thank you." His response was abnormally meek. So much so that Nicola frowned and gave him a suspicious look, but his eyelids had gone down again, and he was lying quietly. She shook her head, annoyed that her imagination was getting out of hand, and tiptoed toward the hall.

Alex opened his eyes to watch her go, and grinned broadly when she rounded the corner.

When Nicola returned a moment or two later, she put her pillow on the other side of the bed and started to take off her robe. Even then, something made her direct a final look at Alex's still form. He was resting with his eyes closed, taking up more than his share of the bed, but it wasn't surprising. He was a tall man, and his shoulders were broad; the sheet which he'd pushed down to his waist revealed that. She wondered if she should have made him button the pajama jacket and leaned across to do it for him. Then she abruptly straightened and dropped her hands. Fortunately, his eyes remained closed, so her action went unnoticed.

Nicola deposited her robe on the end of the bed and slipped under the covers, keeping carefully to her edge. Her hand reached up to switch off the light, and she settled back with a soft sigh.

A moment later it was echoed faintly from the other side of the bed as Alex discovered the truth of the old Roman adage "Man has one thing in view, but Fate often has another."

8

Physical exhaustion took its toll on Alex not long afterward, and he fell into a sound sleep while still considering the frailties of human flesh. It occurred to him that a bridegroom who managed to add a lump on the head to his other infirmities deserved a nonexistent honeymoon. Which was certainly what he was getting. It was on that observation that he fell asleep—unaware that his complaint was not necessarily original.

On the other side of the bed, Nicola was too tired to have any pertinent thoughts. She relaxed in the knowledge that Alex was nearby and probably would feel better in the morning. She just had time to think how much better this bed seemed than the one in the guest room, and made sure she was still on her side of the mattress, before she was sound asleep.

It was the half-muted sound of an alarm which made her stir slightly the next morning. Then the disturbance ceased and she stretched luxuriously under the covers and drowsed off again.

A few minutes later she was caught up in a dream sequence so real that she fully expected to see film credits when it first began. A familiar masculine head appeared on her mental screen—only, Alex wasn't playing the role of a platonic husband any longer. Instead, he was kissing the hollow of her throat in a way that made her turn restlessly on the bed and throw off her covering blanket. Her movements didn't stop him. Alex ignored her feeble protest and pushed aside the thin material covering her shoulder, letting her feel the tip of his tongue as he continued with his lovemaking.

Nicola stirred in her sleep, moving her head languorously on the pillow. She kept her eyes tightly closed until the warmth that enveloped her slowly receded and her breathing returned to normal.

As the tide of confusion ebbed, it was replaced by the stricken realization that she wasn't sleeping alone. Her eyelids flew open, and she sat up, terrified that Alex had noticed.

There was a dent in the pillow on the other side of the bed, but that was the only evidence of another occupant during the night. He'd even straightened the covers after he'd gotten up, so she'd stay warm and comfortable. Nicola's glance swung around the bedroom and then focused on the bathroom, where the door had been left open.

All kinds of catastrophes immediately flashed through her mind. The imagined horrors made her leap out of bed and grab her robe as she tore barefoot out into the hall.

She was trying to open the glass lanai door to see if Alex had collapsed over the railing when she heard the sound of whistling coming from the next room. Relief washed over her, and she left the door ajar as she went to peer in the kitchen. Alex, wearing a navy-blue robe over his pajamas, was apparently surveying the contents of the refrigerator. He was still whistling softly, but her presence must have gotten to him, because he turned and brought his head up sharply, just managing to nick the stainless-steel edge of the freezer compartment on the way.

"Dammit to hell!" he said, glaring at her. "Must you creep around? At this rate, I'll be a basket case."

Recent experience qualified Nicola as a first-aid expert. She dismissed the newest bruise after an appraising glance. "I don't know why you got out of bed. If you were hungry, all you had to do was let me know." Then her eyes narrowed as another possibility occurred to her. "Exactly how long have you been up?"

He turned back to the refrigerator, absently rubbing the tender spot on his head. "Long enough to have a shower and make the coffee. Why? Are we on a schedule?"

"I guess not." His offhand response had made

a mockery of her doubts. It was simply a dream she'd had—nothing more. She endeavored to match his manner. "You look much better, despite your newest injury."

"I'm okay. Just don't ever let my insurance lapse." He pulled out a quarter-pound of butter and frowned at its hardness before putting it on a saucer. "Are you cooking eggs, or am I?"

She waved him away and turned to put on an apron.

He straddled a chair and watched her. "What happened to your slippers? You shouldn't be working around a stove in bare feet."

Nicola stared blankly down at her toes, as if they'd come out of the refrigerator, too. "I forgot to put my slippers on. I was afraid something had happened to you. . . ."

"Like collapsing over the balcony railing?"

"How did you know?"

"I'm getting clairvoyant where you're concerned." He tested the edge of his jaw with his thumb. "How long before breakfast?"

"About ten minutes. Why?"

"Might as well shave if there's time. I'll toss your slippers out to you first." He left the room and returned a little later with them in his hand. "Here . . . put them on," was all he said as he dropped them in the doorway and disappeared again.

By dint of careful timing, Nicola was able to improve her own appearance before he returned. The tiny bathroom off the kitchen allowed her to fix her hair and apply a light touch of lipstick between cooking the sausage and the eggs. A final check in the mirror confirmed that her tailored robe with its satin lapels would be perfectly all right at the breakfast table.

Alex must have thought the same thing when he returned a little later, because his eyebrows went up approvingly as he came in and poured another cup of coffee. By then he had changed into lightweight gray slacks with a matching sport shirt. It was obvious that he wasn't wasting any more time with invalid status, because his first comment was, "What happened to that greenery you were going to get for the lanai? If this light holds, I want to start shooting around noon—provided there's a decent background."

Nicola refused to get upset. She put two slices of bread in the toaster and dished up his breakfast before saying mildly, "The nursery promised delivery this forenoon. I thought that was in plenty of time. Did you tell Juliette that you've moved up the schedule?"

"If I know Juliette, she'll be around." Alex buttered the toast when it popped up, and still found time to assist Nicola with her chair.

"Before I sit down, is anything missing?" she wanted to know, giving the sunlit table a final look.

"Just you." He waved her down, and subsided on his own chair. "This food looks great," he said, picking up his fork. "I'm starving."

"It's easy to see that there's nothing wrong with your appetite." She broke off a piece of toast and took a bite. "You don't plan on working very long today, do you?"

"Depends on how it goes. With any luck, though, we can take in some of the sights around town later. I understand the zoo shouldn't be missed."

"It's great! The koalas alone are worth a special trip. Kevin took me there yesterday."

Nicola was putting jelly on her toast, so she didn't see Alex's annoyed reaction. "How did you happen to get together with Kevin Graham?" he asked. "I thought he was working during the day."

"He said he had the day off. Why? Does it matter?"

"You know what I mean." Alex scowled down at his coffee as if he'd discovered a mosquito floating on the surface. "Most men don't make dates with married women when there's a girlfriend available . . ." He broke off, realizing he was getting in a danger zone.

Nicola didn't wait for him to present it more diplomatically. "You mean Juliette? Kevin complained that she comes on a little strong. I *think* that's how he phrased it."

"I'm sure you'd remember." Alex was watching her through narrowed eyes. "Why didn't he just say that he prefers married women?"

"That's absurd. He knew I was alone, and

probably invited me on the spur of the moment. What could be more platonic than taking a trip to the zoo and a mission?" She would have gone on with her indignant denial except that she suddenly remembered the incident in the mission garden, which wasn't platonic at all.

Her hesitation didn't escape Alex. "What else happened?" he asked in a silky tone.

"Nothing worth talking about. I read somewhere that Winston Churchill and his wife gave up having breakfast together the first week they were married, and I'm beginning to understand why. Anyone would think you were jealous."

Alex slammed his napkin down on the table and shoved his chair back. "There you go jumping to conclusions again! I'm just telling you that if you want to do any more sightseeing, we'll go together. And if Kevin Graham calls with another invitation, he can . . ." He broke off at an insistent buzzing from the next room. "What in the devil's that?"

"The doorbell. If you'd stay home more, you'd recognize it." Nicola said, starting to answer it.

He scowled across the table at her. "Finish your breakfast. I'll get it."

Nicola watched him, aware that their flare-up hadn't done anything for her appetite. She pushed the egg around on her plate for an instant and then scraped it into the garbage. As she rinsed their plates, she was wishing she'd never mentioned her outing with Kevin in the first place. She shook her head, wondering who ever started the rumor that women were the difficult sex.

The sound of activity in the foyer made her peer around the archway to see what was going on. She recognized the dark-haired man from the nursery as he wheeled past a sturdy windmill palm in one of the terra-cotta jardinieres she'd bought.

He greeted her with a smile. " 'Morning, Mrs. Laird. The rest of the order's coming right up. It's on the freight elevator now." He nodded briskly and headed for the lanai door, where Alex was waiting.

Nicola watched the two of them arrange the palm near the end of the railing, and then she disappeared into the bedroom to get dressed.

When she emerged a half-hour later in dark blue slacks and a matching turtleneck sweater, she found that Juliette had already arrived. The model looked very much at home, holding a mug of coffee as she perched on an arm of the davenport and watched Alex adjust his tripod near the lanai door.

Juliette didn't waste any time on elaborate pleasantries with Nicola. "I put my outfits in the guest room. There didn't seem any point in running back and forth to my apartment for changing. Alex said you wouldn't mind."

"Of course not," Nicola murmured quietly. "Would you like anything to go with that coffee?"

"She won't have time," Alex announced. "I want to take advantage of this light while it lasts. Put on the red lounging outfit, Julie. You can drink coffee later."

"I'll take it with me," the model said, getting to her feet and moving unhurriedly down the hallway.

Left alone with Alex, Nicola felt the atmosphere thicken. She was sure it wasn't her imagination, because he moved restlessly around the room instead of dropping easily into the nearest chair as he did in the New York studio when there was extra time.

Nicola found herself fidgeting with the turtleneck on her sweater and made an effort to shove her hands in the pockets of her slacks as she strolled over to the lanai. "Those palms look good," she observed. "I wish we could take them back to New York after this is over. They'd be morale boosters when it starts to snow in Manhattan."

He muttered something in response which prompted her to take a second look at the greenery he'd arranged on the end of the balcony.

"They *are* all right, aren't they?" Nicola wanted to know. "I thought you'd like the containers."

"They're okay." Alex rubbed the back of his head as if it still ached. "I'm not crazy about that painted thing. . . ."

"Which one is that?" She stood on tiptoe for a closer look.

"I shoved it in the back. That pot with the Indian face and the two rings through the ears. It doesn't matter—it won't show in the picture. I don't suppose that you had much choice," he concluded offhandedly.

"Well, I certainly didn't buy anything with earrings. . . ." By then, Nicola was pushing aside the palm fronds to see what he was talking about. "Do you mean this one?" she asked, frowning at a two-foot container in the corner. "I never saw it before. They must have gotten things mixed at the nursery."

"I told you, it doesn't matter." Alex sounded sorry that he'd even brought the matter up. "I should be finished with this a little after twelve. We can have lunch with Juliette and send her on her way. Then we'll spend the afternoon looking around the town. Just the two of us. What's the matter?" He scowled at the uneasy expression on her face. "Doesn't that sound good to you?"

"Normally it would be fine." Nicola tried to choose the right words. "I didn't think you'd be available today, so I made other plans for the afternoon—for lunch, too."

"What kind of plans?" His voice was as tight as the line of his jaw. "Kevin again? You can forget that."

"Don't be absurd," she scoffed. "I'm going fishing."

"You're what?"

"You heard me—I've chartered a boat for the afternoon, and . . ."—she swallowed to regain her bravado—"and I'm going fishing."

"I'll be damned!" Alex was so taken aback that he needed a minute to rally. "What about your work here?"

"There's nothing for me to do when you're shooting. In fact, I'm sure that Juliette will be glad if I disappear."

Alex muttered something profane about Juliette which it was just as well that the model didn't hear.

"That isn't the way you talked about her earlier," Nicola said. She felt a surge of triumph as she went to the closet and put on a navy-blue sweater striped in rust and white.

Alex's expression became suddenly thoughtful. "Is Juliette why you're striking this sudden blow for freedom?"

"I'm not doing anything of the sort—I'm simply taking some time off."

"What about our lunch?"

"Secretaries aren't responsible for employer's lunches these days. That idea went out with Woodrow Wilson." She was looking around for her purse as she spoke.

"You sound like a frustrated sociologist. What's the matter? Don't you like being my secretary any longer?"

His words stung her into telling the truth. "Not particularly."

He sat down on the arm of the davenport that Juliette had occupied earlier, and folded his arms over his chest. "You don't seem to care much for your new job, either. Is that because wives still *do* get lunches for their husbands?"

Sudden color flared to her cheeks. "Real wives, maybe. I'm just an understudy for the weekend, remember? And I don't like pretending." She smoothed the front of her sweater with nervous fingers. "Thank heaven this masquerade won't last much longer. I was a fool to let you talk me into it in the first place. We've done nothing but fight ever since we signed the marriage license." She hesitated and added unhappily, "We never used to argue."

Alex's stern expression softened. "It doesn't have to be an insurmountable obstacle."

"Oh, it's not only that," she went on in a rush. "Nothing's worked out right since we've been here. Even your fishing trip with Pat fizzled. He's the American who's involved with that Chapultepec theft, isn't he?"

"What makes you think that?" Alex asked warily.

"It was obvious. His interest in Maximilian and Carlota. The way he wanted to know what was in your book. Incidentally, I left it in the glove compartment of the car . . . I meant to take it down to the pier when I picked you up." Momentarily she was diverted. "Although I don't see why it matters."

"The Mexican authorities are convinced that

it's one of the few valid accounts of the Empress's jewels. By checking against the treasures that went back to Europe with her, they have a pretty good idea what was in that stolen trunk. They had their theory confirmed by a few jeweled pieces they retrieved in Mexico City, where they found the workman's body."

"And you think Pat Towne was mixed up with the other man later in Puerto Vallarta?"

"I didn't say so. . . ."

"I know." Nicola's lips thinned. "You could have trusted me on that. Among other things," she added, after hearing Juliette call, "Alex . . . I need your help with this zipper," from the bedroom.

"Oh, for lord's sake, Nicola—she's working for me," Alex said, standing up. "Go give her a hand, will you?"

His abrupt order made her temper flare again. "Sorry," she told him flippantly as she headed for the front door. "You can take care of it. I'm tired of Juliette's zippers . . . and I haven't had my coffee break."

His lengthy strides brought him to the door by the time she reached for the knob. "Make sure you recover from all your problems before dinnertime," he said in a soft, dangerous tone. "I'll expect you then, at the latest."

"I don't like ultimatums. . . ."

"And I wouldn't like to notify the Coast

Guard that you're missing, but I sure as hell will if you're not back."

Nicola ground her teeth together so hard that they hurt. "You are the most aggravating, miserable tyrant of a man I've ever come across."

"Alex!" came another pathetic wail from the bedroom.

"Your chum is waiting," Nicola snapped, pulling open the door.

"The hell with that." Alex clamped down on her arm. "An aggravating, miserable tyrant of a husband wouldn't let you go without something else to remember." He yanked her up against him. "If we were alone, this little scene would damned well be staged in the bedroom instead of the front hall."

"Take your hands off me," she said in a furious undertone, trying to get away from his vicelike grip.

"Not until I'm ready," he snarled, pulling her back.

There was an unexpected distraction when Juliette came down the hall. "I'm not going to spend the rest of the day in that bedroom waiting for some help," she said. Her glance focused on their arrested figures. "Am I interrupting anything? Go ahead with what you were doing."

Nicola, her cheeks flaming, managed to escape from Alex's hold and hurried out, slamming the door angrily behind her.

"I hope I didn't spoil anything," Juliette continued, not bothering to hide her amusement as she observed Alex.

"You didn't. We were finished. At least for now." He was still breathing hard.

"It's funny Nicola didn't even say goodbye. . . ."

"Yes, isn't it." He zipped the back of her dress in a matter-of-fact manner and turned toward the living room. "Let's get going on this job."

"Anyone would think you were mad about something," she said, following him.

"You don't get paid to think, honey," he said, not unkindly, as he bent over the camera, "so don't start now."

9

It took considerably longer for Nicola's temper to subside.

She was still muttering dire imprecations about men in general and one male in particular when she reached the lobby entrance. A note in the mailbox caught her attention, and she read the latest communication from Maria. The cramped script said that Ivan's company wasn't needed for the maternity vigil. He was awaiting pickup in the laundry room of the condominium, along with Mr. Laird's clean shirts.

Nicola's lips curved in unholy glee as she read it, and she beckoned to the doorman, who was watching a nurseryman trim fronds from a palm nearby.

"There's a kitten down in the laundry room ..." she began.

"Yes, ma'am. Maria brought him a little while ago." It was clear that he knew all about it.

"Then you'd better take him right up to Mr.

Laird. The poor cat's probably hungry by now. I'm surprised that Maria didn't deliver him in person."

"She wasn't sure how you'd . . ." He broke off and started again more diplomatically. "Maria was pretty rushed. She said she had to get back to her daughter."

"Well, the kitten can't spend the day in the laundry room. I'm sure he'll be much more comfortable in the apartment." Her temper improved as she thought of Ivan sashaying through the middle of a camera session, leaving little cat prints on Juliette's clothes after he'd inspected the dirt in the balcony planters.

Having accomplished all she could for the moment, Nicola started on out toward the car, until she recognized the nurseryman working on the palm and stopped again.

He seemed pleased to see her. "I took care of everything upstairs before I left. Mr. Laird said the plantings looked fine when we got them arranged. I left instructions on how to take care of them—there's a mimeographed sheet on the dining-room table."

"That wasn't what I wanted to talk to you about," she interrupted. "I was wondering where that Indian-head planter came from. The one with the rings in his ears. . . ."

His expression cleared. "Oh, *that* one."

She nodded. "I gather it came from your stock. You don't have to take it back," she added hurriedly. "I was just a little surprised to see it. I knew that I hadn't bought it in Old Town."

"It didn't come from us, Mrs. Laird. That kind of item might sell down in Tijuana, but the people around here don't go for those novelty items. We cater to a different kind of buyer," he added, making it quite clear.

"I see," she said slowly. "Perhaps the man who put the things in my car at Old Town mixed up the order."

"That must have been it." He sounded relieved that she hadn't chosen such an eyesore. "If Mr. Laird wants it replaced, we have a solid brass urn that looks very nice planted with an orange bougainvillea."

"Thanks, I'll tell him," she promised, and nodded as she went on out to the parking lot.

The conversation made her take a careful look in the back of the station wagon when she got in, to see if any other strange souvenirs had been included. The parrot piñata stared cheerfully back at her. Nicola said, "I'll take you upstairs as soon as we come back . . . there's a kitten I know who'd love to make your acquaintance."

The drive out to Quivira Basin was a restful diversion after all that had happened that morning. Nicola had time to spare, and she used some of it having a solitary cup of coffee at a hotel on Harbor Island. A little later she turned onto Nimitz Boulevard and headed directly for the sports-fishing basin adjoining Mission Bay.

There was the usual cluster of parked cars in front of a good-sized modern marina. The complex seemed busier than the one where Pat Towne berthed his boat, and for a moment she wondered just how she'd find the craft she'd hired. But once she'd gotten out of the car and walked around the corner of the building, she saw the charter-boat captain sitting on a locker nearby.

"Right on time," he told her, getting to his feet. "Are you all ready to go?"

"I think so. I wasn't supposed to bring any tackle, was I? You said that you'd supply everything . . ." A thought struck her, and she bit her bottom lip in consternation. "Except that I promised to bring the lunch, and I forgot all about it. Things were a little confused at home. Maybe I can buy some sandwiches in the marina," she said, turning to look over her shoulder.

"Don't give it another thought, Mrs. Laird." He urged her down a wide concrete pier with a small flotilla of fishing boats moored alongside. "My crew brought a lunch, so it's just as well that you forgot about it. And there's always a pot of coffee going in the galley."

"It sounds fine," Nicola assured him. "Probably I'll be too busy fishing to take time out to eat. Is this your boat?" she asked as they drew alongside a thirty-foot cruiser with a bait box on the stern.

"That's it." For an instant the man looked a little uncertain. Then he went on with a forced air of heartiness. "Actually, I've had to change things around a little. One of my men can't take his regular shift at the marina, and I have to help out. I didn't want to disappoint you, though," he put in hastily, "so a friend of mine volunteered to take this trip. He knows what he's doing—as a matter of fact, he's a better fisherman than I am, though I usually don't go around admitting it. All you have to do is climb aboard."

"All right." Nicola lingered a minute longer. "Is he here now?"

"Sure thing." He nodded toward the bridge, where a man's silhouette was visible, "And he's all set to go. I told him La Jolla would be far enough. That'll get you back here well before dinnertime."

Nicola couldn't think of any other reasons for hesitating, so she let him assist her over the rail of the boat and braced herself against the bait box while he cast off the stern line. Then he moved quickly along the dock to do the same at the bow, and gave a genial dismissal to the figure up in the cabin.

There was the sudden noise of powerful engines being throttled back as the cruiser reversed neatly from the slip and came about, heading toward the ocean.

A brisk breeze whipped Nicola's hair across her face, and she pulled a scarf out of her sweater pocket, tying it over her head. The sudden tilt of the deck as the cruiser turned into the main channel made her clutch the side of the open bait tank for support. Three small anchovies were flopping feebly on the rim of the tank, gasping to stay alive in the water which occasionally splashed over them. Nicola bent down and hastily pushed them in the deep marine tank. A minute later she saw them revive and dart among the others crowding the water. The ramifications of fishing with live bait hadn't made any impression on her until then. She was frowning as she turned and made her way forward toward the wheelhouse.

As she drew abreast of the open door, Pat Towne greeted her with a mocking grin. "I wondered when you'd come up and say hello."

"You! What in the world are you doing here?"

"Taking you fishing," he said, enjoying her astonishment. "There's a stool behind you, if you want to stay awhile."

Nicola became aware that her mouth was hanging open much like the poor anchovies who were on the side of the bait box. She brought her lips together and stared at the tall figure handling the wheel. "I gather this wasn't a coincidence," she said finally.

"That all depends on how you look at things. 'Opportunity' is a better word. I was really surprised when you showed up alone at the marina; I didn't think Alex would approve of that. Not from the way he talked the other day."

Nicola was torn between an urge to know exactly what Alex had said and a reluctance to discuss her private life. "I didn't know that Alex would be back when I made these arrangements," she said, "and he had a shooting schedule this morning that couldn't be postponed."

"With Juliette?"

"That's right. She's the model hired for this account. Probably he told you about that, too."

Pat spun the wheel as they reached the end of the breakwater, where brown pelicans perched on the rocks, and turned the cruiser north into the choppy waves of the Pacific. "I hope this motion doesn't bother you," he said, noticing the way she hung on to the cabin door as he increased speed. "It'll be better when we get a little farther out. Then we can anchor and take life easy."

Nicola nodded, happy to discover that she didn't feel any symptoms of queasiness. Unfortunately, while that worry had disappeared, her sense of anticipation toward the day's outing had gone along with it. The prospect of lounging on the stern of a fishing boat in the sunshine seemed suddenly lackluster.

"Have you had anything to eat?" Pat wanted to know.

She shook her head. "I'm not really hungry."

"Well, I am. If you go down in the galley and
pour a couple of cups of coffee, I'll join you
with the lunch, once we've anchored." He
jerked his head toward a sturdy paper bag
wedged next to the depth meter under the
cabin window.

"How do you know where to anchor?" she
asked, hesitating in the doorway to watch him
scan the water ahead of them.

"You can see where the birds are feeding, for
one thing—except for those pelicans hanging
around the bait barges. Or I take a look in the
crystal ball," he said, pointing to the depth indicator. "That shows the bottom conditions and
schools of fish. After that, I read my day's horo-
scope."

It was impossible not to respond to his grin.
"I'll get the coffee," Nicola said lightly. "You'll
find me out on the afterdeck when you bring the
food."

While making her way to the tiny galley, she
was deciding that Alex must have been mis-
taken in his suspicions of the tall, fair-haired
fishing captain. As far as she could tell, Pat had
little on his mind other than a lazy afternoon of
fishing. Probably that was the only reason he'd
volunteered for the job. And as for his interest
in Mexican history—she could bring that into
the conversation during the trip to see what she
could learn. The possibility of earning Alex's
gratitude and admiration later on made her
glow.

It wasn't long afterward that she heard the throb of the engines die away and felt the cruiser wallow roughly before settling on its anchor chain.

She came out of the galley carrying two mugs of coffee, to find Pat already arranging chairs near the stern.

He looked up and grinned. "Is sitting in the sunshine all right with you? Might as well take advantage of the weather while we can."

Nicola nodded, handing him his coffee. "From the looks of your tan, you've already spent a lot of time in the sun."

"You know how it is on the water." He put his coffee on a corner of the bait box for easy access, paying no attention to an anchovy still flopping in the gunwale near his foot.

"Look out! You'll step on him," Nicola warned, starting to get up and rescue it.

"What? Oh, that!" Towne ground the fish carelessly under his heel and then kicked the remains over the rail. "We'll never miss it. The box is full of them."

Nicola subsided in her chair again, feeling a twinge of revulsion at his action. She shook her head when he hauled over the bag of sandwiches. "No, thanks. Not right now. I had a late breakfast."

"Suit yourself." He was unwrapping his, plainly unaware of her feelings. "There's cheese or ham—I thought you'd prefer that to sardines or tuna fish."

Nicola's stomach muscles tightened, and she took a hasty swallow of coffee before directing her gaze toward the shoreline. "Is that La Jolla over there?"

"The business section's a little farther north." He shifted in his chair. "I hope you're not expecting great things from the fishing out here, especially in a transitional season like this. We can try for a surface catch, but I don't think there'll be much luck."

"You've lost me already," she confessed.

He looked amused. "Mackerel . . . bonito . . . yellowtail. Does that help?"

"A little." Nicola was glad that her stomach had decided to settle down again and behave itself. "What did you and Alex go for on your Mexican trip?"

"I thought there might be some tuna, but bonito was what we ended up with. That husband of yours wasn't happy. Didn't even seem to enjoy Ensenada very much." Pat looked at her as he took a swallow of coffee. "I got the feeling he was missing you."

"You're just a romantic at heart. He was probably thinking about the big one that got away."

"There weren't many of those. Say, that reminds me. I wanted to thank you for storing that stuff in the marina for me. My client was down to pick it up this morning."

Nicola started to tell him about the trouble

she'd had getting it stowed away and then decided it wasn't worth bothering about.

Pat was going on. "Alex didn't send that book on Maximilian and Carlota along with you this morning, did he?"

Nicola gave him a puzzled look. "How could he? I didn't know I was even meeting you. But as a matter of fact . . ." She was going to say that she still had the book in the glove compartment of the station wagon when something in his intent glance made her hesitate. After all, it was Alex's book to lend—not hers.

"You were saying?" There was no disguising the interest in his voice.

Nicola stalled. "I'm sorry. What was I talking about?"

"That book on the Empress Carlota."

"Of course." She gave him an apologetic smile. "I'll have to ask Alex where it is. He must have put it in a drawer someplace. If you're finished eating, maybe you could show me what I do now."

His features relaxed, but he was still watching her closely. "I gather that you're talking about fishing."

Nicola kept her gaze wide-eyed. "Of course. I even thought that I'd supply Alex with fish for dinner. Was that wrong?"

"Well, I know a Chinese restaurant at Point Loma where they do a great shark-fin soup," he said, getting up. His sardonic expression showed that he recognized her evasive tactic, but the businesslike way he reached for the rods clamped next to the cabin indicated that he'd go along with the game.

Nicola had trouble keeping a straight face; an unsteady boat deck which reeked of fish fell far short of a mission garden when it came to staging a pass—even a halfhearted one. Probably that was one reason there were so many fishing widows left ashore, she decided, and wondered if Alex could be weaned to another hobby before it was too late.

"This is twenty-pound line with a two-gang setup on it," Pat was saying as he put a bamboo rod in her hand. "I'll pull your chair over to the rail so you can be comfortable."

"No, I'd rather stand up . . . if you don't mind." She was staring at the reel. "What do I do with that?"

"You let out the line." Pat was having trouble holding on to his patience. "Keep your thumb on it until you hit bottom, then reel up about four inches. I don't think it's any use even trying to fish the surface."

"Whatever you say." Obediently she turned toward the rail.

"Wait a minute. You have to put on some bait. The fish aren't *that* hard up around here."

She swung back, frowning. "What do I use for bait?"

"An anchovy, of course." He lowered his voice with an effort. "That's what the bait tanks are for."

Nicola wasn't going down to defeat without a struggle. "You mean I have to kill one of those little things first?" She started to put down her rod. "No way."

"How do you suppose people catch fish around here? Even the environmentalists haven't raised any objections. Besides, you just put an anchovy on the hook—you don't need to kill it."

Nicola went over and surveyed the tank of small silver fish. Then she looked at the hooks on the end of her line, and finally back to Pat. "I simply can't do it."

"All right, *I'll* do it," he said, grabbing her pole so impatiently that the hooks swung dangerously close to his thumb. "You just look the other way, and I'll make sure of the rest."

Nicola subsided meekly. Pat took no chances after he'd baited her hooks, casting the line out over the stern and then bringing the rod around to her.

"Now . . . wait for a jerk. Then reel in fast, but keep it steady. Got that?" He sounded as if he understood why Alex hadn't invited her fishing before.

She nodded, somewhat abashed but still of the same mind, no matter what he thought.

When the minutes went by and nothing happened, she relaxed slightly and looked around, to see Pat in the same position, with his rod over the other side of the boat.

"No luck?" His tone had softened. "Sometimes it takes a while. You don't have to worry about talking—not when you have that much line out."

"I didn't have anything to say."

He mistakenly interpreted that for an apology. "Don't worry," he said magnanimously, "you'll get used to all this. Some of the best charter customers I have are women. San Diego gets a lot of them—even from the East Coast. They like Baja and the climate out here. There were quite a few who came out to get a Mexican divorce and went fishing at the same time.

Nicola's eyebrows climbed.

"You don't have to look so disapproving," he said, noting her reaction. "That's all over now. Since the Mexicans have clamped down on their divorce laws, the women just come for fishing."

A strange feeling that had nothing to do with the motion of the boat made Nicola's stomach muscles tighten again. "I don't understand. What do you mean about the Mexicans and their divorce laws?"

"Just that a Mexican marriage is as binding as any performed in the States these days. The Tijuana divorce marts went out of business a few years ago. The courts down there won't touch alien divorce litigation." He stared at her in consternation. "What's the matter—don't you feel well?"

"I feel fine." Her words came out with an effort.

"You look as if somebody had hit you over the head. Maybe it's the sun. Or maybe you should have eaten something."

"It's not that." Nicola cast about for a reason to sit down and think things over. Important things like how Alex would react when he learned that an overnight Mexican divorce was now out of the question.

"Anybody would suspect that you'd been planning a weekend in Tijuana to shed your husband while you were here," Pat said with heavy-handed humor. "Well, don't try it. He knows better."

Nicola froze, still in her position by the rail. "You mean you discussed it with him?"

"We talked about their customs and laws on that first fishing trip before you arrived. I guess he was interested in modern Mexico as well as the historical side."

"You're sure?" Nicola had to be absolutely certain he was telling the truth before she gave in to the warm feeling that was spreading through her.

"Positively." He came over beside her. "Look out for your rod! You almost let it slip through your fingers for a minute there. Did you get a bite?"

"A bite?" Nicola had trouble coming back to reality from a world that suddenly offered possibilities beyond her wildest dreams. She stared down at the rod in her hands and then back up at Pat. "You mean a fish?"

He rubbed his forehead as if it ached. "I sure as hell didn't mean a mosquito. Maybe you'd better reel in. That's the round thing with the handle."

She did as he asked, ignoring his sarcasm. Just then all she wanted was to get back to the apartment and talk to Alex about the things she hoped to hear.

"Reel it smoothly—don't jerk the line," Pat cautioned, hovering over her.

"It doesn't matter," she said, still bringing it in, "but if you don't mind, I'd like to cut the trip short and go on back to the marina."

"I *thought* you looked under the weather." Pat shot her an anxious glance and reached for her rod. "I'll do that for you—you should have told the truth earlier."

"The feeling just hit me," she confessed, trying to look suitably infirm. "It certainly takes a long time to get in all the line, doesn't it?" Her eyes widened as the end finally broke the surface. "For Pete's sake—what's that?"

"That . . . is a fish," Towne said. He brought it over the rail, to flop feebly on the deck. "God knows how long you've had it on the hook. Didn't you feel anything?"

Nicola shook her head and stared down at the long, orangish-red specimen with distaste. "I liked the anchovies better. This thing looks like something on a closeout table at the fish market."

"It's a salmon grouper," Pat said indignantly. "And a pretty good-sized one, at that."

Nicola wrinkled her nose. "Put him back."

"Some people like to eat them."

"Some people like to eat chocolate-covered grasshoppers. Put him back in the water, will you?" She watched as Pat removed the hook and tossed the fish overboard. "Thanks—that's better. Before we go back in, tell me one more thing," she said, walking over to store her rod in a clip on the cabin wall. "Did I buy those anchovies in the bait box?"

Pat nodded as he went over to put his rod above hers. "I'm 'way ahead of you. You want them back in the briny, too."

"Only if they're my property."

Pat reached for a dip net without replying. It took him four scoops before he was finished and the last anchovy flipped into the sea. "Now you know how Lincoln felt," he told Nicola as he put the dripping net down again and reached in his shirt pocket for a cigarette. "And I'll have another chapter when I write my memoirs on this screwball business. Want to go back?"

"Yes, please."

"Okay." He started toward the cabin, and then turned to say over his shoulder, "Don't get any ideas about liberating that last sandwich. I have plans of my own for that."

It was forty-five minutes later before they were back in their berth at the marina.

Nicola waited until a dockhand had secured

their mooring lines and Pat had cut the engines before she went up to the wheelhouse to say good-bye.

"Thanks for trying," she said, holding out her hand. "I promised to take up something simpler next time—like water polo."

He captured her fingers in a firm grasp and made no attempt to release them. "I don't know anything about water polo, but I give scuba lessons in my free time, and I'd be glad to take you on."

"I'll keep it in mind." She pulled gently on her hand, until he released it. "I'm sorry I was such a nuisance today, but then, you owed me something."

His glance sharpened. "Oh? How's that?"

"I wasn't going to tell you, but I had trouble getting rid of that cargo your last customer left aboard. I had to keep it in the back of Alex's car overnight. Ouch! What are you doing?" The last came in a yelp of pain as he caught her wrist in a tight grip.

"When that stuff was in the car, could anything have been taken?"

"I suppose it's possible." She tried to pull away. "Let go of me, will you?"

"Sorry." He didn't sound apologetic as he stood looking down at her. "You didn't notice anything missing?"

"I didn't pay any attention. One man at the marina loaded the car, and another one unloaded it the next day."

"And nothing happened in between?"

She bit her lip as she concentrated. "Not that I can remember. Oh, wait a minute—I did make one stop. At the nursery near the apartment. I'd bought some containers that Alex wanted planted with palms for the lanai." A sudden thought struck her. "Your customer didn't have an Indian-head urn in his stuff, did he?"

"What do you know about that?" Pat's fingers tightened on her wrist.

"I'm not going to say any more," she said, trying to keep her voice steady as pain shot up her arm. "You can ask Alex if you have any more questions,"

"Don't worry. He'll come in for his share. Where are your car keys?" His glance went down to the small pouch she'd tucked under her belt. "Give 'em here," he instructed her.

"I don't know what this is all about . . ."

"You'll find out in time," he said in a level voice that was all the more frightening because it was so carefully controlled. "If you want to keep this arm out of a cast," he advised, "you'll follow orders without arguing."

Nicola hesitated only an instant longer. Then she fished in her leather pouch with her free hand and drew out her key ring.

"That's the girl." His grip loosened so that it was no longer painful, but he didn't make any pretense of releasing her. "Show me where you're parked, and we'll go on a little ride." As she started toward the marina entrance, he shook his head. "Not that way. We'll take a shortcut through here."

Nicola did as he asked, because there was no alternative. As she walked across the parking lot toward the station wagon, she wondered why the marina had to be completely deserted just then.

Her thoughts must have been easy to read, because Pat gave a snort of amusement. "It's too early for the charters to be coming in. You couldn't have picked a better time for me if you'd tried." He motioned for her to unlock the door on the passenger side. "Now, slide under the wheel. I'll be right here beside you, so don't try anything foolish." His big hand clamped warningly around the back of her neck. "Get the idea?"

"It isn't difficult."

"Then we might as well enjoy our ride back to Coronado," he said, motioning for her to turn on the ignition. "You can drive straight to the nursery and get that vase back for me."

"But they don't have it . . ." Her words broke off as she felt his fingers tighten. "That's the truth," she added desperately.

"Then where is it?" His eyebrows came together in an ominous line as she hesitated. "Your apartment's the only other place it could be. How much does Alex know about this?" he asked.

"He doesn't know anything. I mean it," she

went on earnestly. "He thinks I bought the vase in Old Town. All he did was complain about the design."

"Then there won't be any trouble getting it back, will there? You can go in and just tell him that you made a mistake at the nursery. I'll be along to carry out the merchandise."

Nicola almost blurted that he'd need muscles like the Jolly Green Giant to move the container plus the five-foot palm tree planted in it, but caution kept her silent. There was no point in spelling things out for the man beside her. Not when she realized that he couldn't risk leaving witnesses, once he'd recovered his property.

Towne tightened his fingers cruelly, to bring her back to the present. "Step on that accelerator! I don't want to take all afternoon getting to Coronado. That's enough," he warned as the dashboard indicator rose. "Keep it on the speed limit, and don't attract any attention."

Again, Nicola followed his orders, because there was no other choice. Traffic was thready at that hour, and there wasn't even a fleeting glimpse of a patrol car on the entire length of the freeway.

When they crossed the bridge to Coronado and stopped at the toll booth, Towne had the exact change ready. He didn't relax until they were safely beyond it, then he rubbed his thumb caressingly under her ear. "I like a woman who follows orders. It's too bad that you insisted on fishing while we were out on that boat. I had some other things in mind." As Nicola continued to stare straight ahead, he gave a short, cynical laugh. "You've been trouble in more ways than one. I don't often misjudge a woman, but I had you pegged all wrong." His voice sharpened as he leaned forward. "What's all the commotion over there in the parking lot by the condominium?"

Nicola's hopes went up at the sight of some uniformed men surrounding two limousines and a van near the hotel, until she recognized them. "There's nothing to get excited about," she said flatly. "A TV crew is shooting a pilot film over at the Del Coronado. They have been there most of the week."

"What about those cops?"

"The television people hire them on their off-duty hours to help with the crowds and equipment."

"Well, I'm not taking any chances. Park in that empty space in the middle of the lot." He waited until she followed his direction, and then reached over to remove the ignition key. "Now, get out on your side. And remember— I'm right behind you."

They had taken just half a dozen steps toward the condominium when one of the older policemen standing by the equipment van hurried across the lot toward them. "Hey—you there! Just a minute!"

"Hell!" Towne muttered under his breath, and dropped his hand to rest atop Nicola's shoulders. "Remember what I told you." He bit out the warning even as he turned to face the uniformed officer. "Is something wrong?"

"You can't park over there. That space has been reserved for the film company's use. You'll have to move the station wagon right now." He put his hands on his hips and waited for them to turn back.

Nicola didn't hesitate. She flashed a brilliant smile and said, "Pat, you have the keys. Be a dear and move it, will you? I'll meet you upstairs." She pulled sideways as she spoke and slithered out of Towne's grasp. For that moment, he was helpless under the policeman's truculent stare, and Nicola fled toward the apartment doorway while she had the chance.

Once in the lobby, she looked around frantically for a security man—anyone—who could help, but the reception area, like the marina in Mission Bay, loomed emptily around her. An instant later she rushed into the elevator and pressed the button, hoping for better luck on the sixth floor.

Once there, she raced down the hall, all set to pound on the apartment door before she discovered that it was already ajar. She pushed into the foyer as if the fiends of hell were hot on her heels, slamming the door shut and then sliding the bolt with shaking fingers.

Only then did she turn around to search for Alex.

Instead, she found Kevin Graham staring at her with alarm from the lanai. "What in the devil's going on?" he wanted to know. "That entrance of yours startled me so that I almost went over the railing." He jerked his head toward the balcony behind him. "Do you always come into a room like that?"

Nicola shook her head, staying slumped against the door as she tried to control her breathing. "Where's Alex?" she managed finally.

"He got a phone call and went out about five minutes ago," Kevin said, watching her from across the room. He was dressed in sport clothes, but there was nothing relaxed in his manner. His next question showed it. "What's happened? You look—"

"I *know* how I look," Nicola cut in, too upset to be polite. "You don't have to tell me." She started toward the phone at the end of the davenport. "Is there an emergency number for the police?"

He moved swiftly to cut her off. "Wait a minute. Tell me what happened first. Maybe it's something one of our security guards can handle."

"Well, then, for lord's sake, call one," she said in a high, thin tone. "A charter-boat captain named Pat Towne will be here any minute—

that policeman in the parking lot won't keep him long. I'd better make sure the service door is double-bolted, too."

Kevin's arm shot out to stop her when she would have darted toward the kitchen. "The hell with that! I know who Pat Towne is, but what's he coming here for?"

Her hands went out in exasperation. "A planter—of all things. A nasty-looking planter that the nursery found in the back of our station wagon. I didn't even realize the switch was made until Alex pointed it out this morning."

"You mean Alex knew about it, too?"

"What is there to know?" She ran a distracted hand over her forehead. "Oh, my lord, I'm not even sure if it's still on the lanai. Call the police while I go and see." She pulled out of his grip and hurried toward the balcony.

The scene that met her eyes made her pull up beside the half-open sliding door.

The Indian-head container lay on its side on the lanai floor, with the palm that the nursery had planted so carefully halfway out of the top. Dirt and peat moss were scattered all around it. Whoever had tried to unearth the tree had been working in frantic haste.

Nicola felt grit under her shoe, and the sound triggered another memory. Her glance moved abruptly to her arm where Kevin had caught hold of her, leaving a smudge of the same grit.

She wheeled to face the building manager,

who stood by the telephone, noticing for the first time the telltale peat-moss particles clinging to the knees of his trousers. As her expression changed, he smiled and brushed his hands together deliberately. "So now you know," he said.

"You mean you're in it, too?" Nicola felt as if she'd wandered into a nightmare where there was no escape. "You and Pat were together in it—whatever it is." A sudden thought helped her sort it out. "The cargo from his boat belonged to you, didn't it? You were the customer he'd taken on that last fishing trip." She looked toward the balcony in bewilderment. "But why didn't you just say that you wanted the urn back? I didn't mean to keep it. It isn't as if it's a work of art or anything . . ." Her voice dropped as he purposefully moved toward her. "Is it a work of art?" Her last words came out in a whisper.

"Hell, no! It's worth about five dollars at the most."

"Then why . . . ?"

"Ask your husband—I'm sure he can give you all the answers. I can't waste any more time." He grabbed her arm and twisted it savagely behind her back as he pushed her toward the hall closet. "You're lucky that you're dealing with me instead of Pat. He doesn't like leaving people around."

Nicola struggled to escape as she saw him pick up a sharp-edged onyx ashtray on the way.

He seemed to enjoy her terror. "Who knows? After you've had a little nap," he went on smoothly, "you may decide that you don't have anything left to say."

At that moment Nicola realized that she'd have more chance with Pat Towne than the ruthless man beside her. If Kevin hit her with that ashtray, she'd be lucky to ever open her eyes again.

The thought made her knees buckle, throwing him momentarily off balance. Even then, the movement wouldn't have had any effect if the phone hadn't rung at the same time. Kevin instinctively turned toward the sound, shifting his grip as he moved.

Nicola jerked loose and fled toward the front door, scrabbling at the knob like someone demented. Footsteps thudded behind her, and she felt his hand yank at her shoulder as she got the door free. The force of his motion had a chain effect; the door careened open, with Nicola still clutching the knob like a second skin.

She started to scream, and ducked to ward off a blow from behind, when she felt Kevin's body stiffen. Then she heard the crash of the heavy ashtray breaking on the slate at her feet, and she half-turned, to see Alex and another man advancing in a murderous rush.

It happened so suddenly that Nicola was defenseless in Kevin's grasp when his body gave way before the onslaught. Her head was slammed back, catching the edge of the open door with painful and unerring accuracy.

She sagged to the floor without a sound. There wasn't even time to reflect that the ashtray hadn't been needed, after all.

10

The next time Nicola came fully awake was later that night.

In the interim, she experienced considerable confusion, with Kevin, Pat, and Alex appearing in her thoughts at disjointed intervals. Then an elderly gray-haired stranger had come forth with soothing words about closing her eyes and going to sleep.

She cooperated so wholeheartedly that darkness had fallen by the time she stirred and finally woke up. It took an instant longer before she recognized Alex's tall figure sitting on the edge of the bed beside her. There was enough illumination from the bathroom to see that he was wearing a robe belted around his waist but very little else.

A moment later she found out why. Apparently she had been draped in his pajama coat sometime during her lengthy nap. She pushed up on an elbow and discovered that whoever had performed the task hadn't bothered to button it. "Why am I wearing this?" she asked, scowling.

"You had to wear something," Alex said matter-of-factly. "The doctor took a look at you and said to put you to bed."

Nicola touched the swollen spot on the back of her head and winced. "I'm beginning to remember." Then she frowned again. "Except about the doctor."

"That's not surprising. You weren't awake at the time." Alex leaned back on his hand to get comfortable. "He's a tenant here in the building. Very obliging man. Came right down when I called."

"I see." Nicola wasn't sure that she entirely approved, so she chose more familiar territory. "That's all very well . . . but I'd prefer my own pajamas—now that the emergency is over." She also wanted to ask who had put her in the pajama top, but it seemed safer to ignore ancient history.

"Don't blame you a bit. You look like you're wrapped in a shroud." Alex yawned and got to his feet. "Take it off, and I'll get the pills the doctor left." He headed for the bathroom, without a backward glance.

Nicola felt a moment of triumph as she slipped off the oversized top and pulled the sheet around her as she waited for his return. Once in her own pajamas, it would be easier to maintain a semblance of dignity. For the first time, she'd meet him on equal terms instead of starting out at a disadvantage.

Alex came back into the room and handed her a small bottle of pills before removing the offending pajama coat to the closet.

Nicola was reading the label on the medicine bottle. "Repeat the treatment ás necessary." She looked up, frowning, as he returned. "What are they for?"

"Just mild sedation. The main idea is to keep you relaxed for the next day or so. The doctor was sure you'd be back to normal in no time at all. How do you feel now?" he asked, standing over her.

"Not bad," she admitted, giving him the bottle to put on the bed table and absently hitching the sheet higher. Belatedly she discovered that he'd forgotten to bring her pajamas.

Even as she started to mention it, Alex yawned and sat down on the foot of the bed, saying, "I'll bet that Kevin Graham has one hell of a headache now that he's had time to think things over in jail. Especially if Pat Towne's in an adjoining cell. They were both screaming for a lawyer, but the Mexican government's angling for extradition on them so they'll have to stay behind bars until the red tape is sorted out."

Nicola arranged the pillow behind her, loath to miss a thing. "But how did you know they were involved? Kevin said you'd gone out of the building earlier."

"That's what we wanted him to think. I

ducked out the front door and came back in the service entrance with Marco."

"Your Mexican friend from Chapultepec?"

Alex nodded. "He'd come up here to be in at the finish of the case. The Mexican authorities were sure that Towne and Graham were guilty, but they needed actual proof."

"You didn't say anything to me about Kevin being involved," Nicola accused. Then her expression cleared as she said, "That's why you were so annoyed when I went out with him."

"It's one reason." Alex bestowed a cynical glance from his end of the bed. "I swear to God you'd have been helping Jack the Ripper sharpen knives a hundred years ago. I never saw such a woman for getting into trouble."

"You were the one who invited me to San Diego," she pointed out. "Can I help it if things happened?"

"That's an understatement if I ever heard one!" He shook his head slightly. "Okay—so I'm partially to blame. But why in hell did you have to go fishing with Pat Towne today?"

"Oh . . . that!" It was so long ago that Nicola had to stop and think. "Honestly, I didn't make the arrangement with him originally."

"We discovered that later. Otherwise you'd never have been allowed to leave this apartment. And just for the record—I'll teach you all you need to know about fishing from now on."

Since this was exactly what Nicola had hoped, she gave a pleased wriggle, which almost dislodged her sheet. She tucked it around her again and said, "I was certainly glad to see that off-duty policeman in the parking lot. Pat had me petrified by then."

"I can imagine. You might feel better to know that that policeman was doing just what he was ordered to do. The authorities had Towne under surveillance all along. They were convinced that he was responsible for the disappearance of the man in Puerto Vallarta, and they suspected that once he had the treasure, he'd need a market for it. That's why Kevin came in as his partner. He was the distribution man responsible for fencing the merchandise. Marco thinks that they shifted the stuff a little at a time, whenever Pat took his boat down below the border on a charter. We found a whole row of those Indian-head planters around the swimming pool just outside Kevin's office. Right now, they're down at headquarters, too."

"But why didn't the nurserymen find anything when they planted the palm tree?"

"It wasn't that simple. The various pieces were sandwiched into the clay before the urn went into the kiln."

Nicola's eyes were wide as she thought about it. "Then you were right about how your book came into the scheme of things. Pat really wanted to get his hands on it."

Alex's grin was cynical. "So I heard. You did a neat shell game there—keeping it in the station wagon instead of the apartment."

"Oh, that! It was pure luck."

"That wasn't the term Towne used when we told him where it was. He had wanted to double-check the evaluation of Carlota's jewelry to make sure that Kevin and the fence didn't shortchange him. I imagine Kevin wanted to take possession of the book for just the opposite reason."

Nicola chewed thoughtfully on her thumbnail. "One thing I don't understand—how did Kevin learn that the vase was here in the apartment?"

"There weren't many places you could have taken it, so probably he just asked around. Juliette was the most logical person to tell him. He could have questioned her after the modeling session this morning and confirmed the fact with the nursery. Afterward, he used the rental agreement as an excuse for dropping in to the apartment. When I pretended to duck out later, it gave him the perfect chance to investigate."

"But what if you'd come back unexpectedly?"

"I imagine he planned to brazen it out. He could have said he'd knocked the urn over by accident, and would have offered to take it with him and have it replanted."

"He had lots of fast answers," Nicola admitted. Fortunately, she missed Alex's sudden scowl when he remembered their afternoon at the zoo. An afternoon that could have been disastrous.

"I'm sorry you got involved in any of it," he said gruffly. "It never occurred to Marco and me that you'd come up to the apartment this afternoon. That policeman was supposed to hang on to you as well as Towne."

"I didn't give him a chance." Nicola was matter-of-fact. "Besides, it's worth having a headache—just to know that it's all over. I'll bet that Kevin was responsible for searching our belongings that first night."

"I'm sure of it. I'd been asking too many questions of Pat."

"And the man who made that strange phone call?"

"I doubt if we'll ever learn the truth about that." Alex got to his feet and stretched hugely. "It's late, and you can use some more sleep." He went over to turn out the bathroom light after opening the drapes enough to let moonlight filter in.

Nicola was going to protest that she had no intention of being shunted off to sleep again, when she noticed that Alex wasn't heading toward the guest room but was circling back to the other side of the bed. "You're staying here?" she finally managed to ask.

He turned back the covers on his side. "I've been here all along," he said, shrugging off his robe and calmly getting between the sheets. "Ivan's sleeping it off in the guest bedroom. I thought he needed a sedative too, so I gave him that jar of strained beef. He was so full, he could barely make it to the bed."

"Oh."

Alex didn't appear to notice her faint monosyllable. Instead he shoved his pillow into place and went on conversationally, "I thought we might take Ivan home with us when we go. We need a better souvenir than those two tiles we bought in Tijuana, and he'd provide a real challenge for William."

Nicola, who knew that the old retainer polished the furniture every day, stifled a giggle. "I think it's a wonderful idea if Ivan doesn't start sharpening his claws on the Hepplewhite. William has his work cut out for him."

Alex turned to look at her for the first time since he'd gotten into bed. "He's not the only one," he said somewhat ruefully, "but we'll talk about it another time. The doctor left orders for me to keep you relaxed and in a good frame of mind tonight."

Nicola wondered for a giddy moment just how he planned to accomplish all that. If he contemplated turning his back on her and going to sleep, he'd have a rebellion on his hands. She was trying to think of a discreet, ladylike way of getting her point across, when Alex solved the problem.

With one masterful sweep of his arm, she was hauled over and settled comfortably against him.

When Nicola encountered the cool, hard strength of Alex's thigh pressed against hers, she felt a languor steal over her body that she'd never known before. It was intensified when his hands moved over her with gentle, sure possession, and when he leaned down to kiss her, Nicola's heartbeat thundered like a coastal storm.

The discovery that his pulse was racing just as fast gave her courage to lay her head on his chest and say, "Pat told me about Mexican divorces this afternoon. Apparently they aren't easy for Americans to get these days. You were wrong about that."

His chuckle was deep and convincing. "The devil I was. I knew exactly what I was doing when I lured you across the border, Mrs. Laird." The last two words were muffled, because he'd abandoned her lips and was searching for new fields to conquer. He went on a little later, when talking was possible again. "I'd been looking for a chance to marry you for the last six months. I was sick and tired of being paired off with every new model that came into the studio."

Nicola's head came up at that. "It didn't look like it. Not with a different order for the florist every week." She could feel his laughter, and relaxed against him once again. "All right—so I was jealous. I wanted to scratch their eyes out."

"I thought you were fraying a little at the edges." He sounded supremely satisfied. "That's why I wanted you out here, and when I saw an excuse to get married . . . it was too good to turn down. I just hoped that you wouldn't know how binding a Mexican marriage ceremony really was. Not then. I planned to tell you afterward."

His words reminded him of something else that he'd been trying to ignore for the past few minutes. He sighed and gently moved away from his wife's inviting figure. "There'll be plenty of time to talk about it later, dearest. You have about as much chance of getting rid of me . . ." He swallowed and shook his head as words failed him. "Anyhow, don't get any ideas."

"I haven't had a rational thought since you got into this bed," she admitted.

"Darling, I'm sorry," he apologized. "God knows what the doctor would say. Turn over and get some sleep now. The important thing is for you to get well."

She put a hand on his shoulder when he would have moved away.

"What is it?" He raised up on an elbow and looked at her with concern. "Are you feeling worse? I'll get you one of those pills—"

She put her fingers to his lips and effectively stopped his words. "I don't need a pill," she said, pushing him back down to the mattress again. "But I do have a complaint." Her finger feathered across his chest in a way that made him draw in his breath.

"Keep that up, my love," he warned softly, "and you'll be missing some more sleep. I've been wanting you so long that I shouldn't be in the same room with you—let alone the same bed."

She stared innocently back at him, but the lilt in her voice revealed all he wanted to know. "I can't understand why you're feeling guilty," she said. "The doctor told you what to do, and even the label on his prescription says to 'Repeat the treatment as necessary.'"

Her laughter stopped abruptly when she was pulled back against him with one decisive movement. Then there was just time for her to realize how much she loved him before his lips came down and parted hers.

About the Author

Glenna Finley is a native of Washington State. She earned her degree from Stanford University in Russian Studies and in Speech and Dramatic Arts, with emphasis on radio.

After a stint in radio and publicity work in Seattle, she went to New York City to work for NBC as a producer in its international division. In addition, she worked with the "March of Time" and *Life* magazine.

As a producer, she had her own show about activities in Manhattan, a show that was broadcast to England. The programs were similar to those of the "Voice of America."

Though her life in New York was exciting, she eventually returned to the Northwest where she married. Currently residing in Seattle with her husband, Donald Witte, and their son, she loves to travel, and draws heavily on her travels and experiences for the novels that have been published. Her books for NAL have sold several million copies.

SIGNET Books You'll Want to Read

- [ ] **ALLEGRA by Clare Darcy.** (#E7851—$1.75)
- [ ] **ELYZA by Clare Darcy.** (#E7540—$1.75)
- [ ] **LADY PAMELA by Clare Darcy.** (#W7282—$1.50)
- [ ] **LYDIA by Clare Darcy.** (#W6938—$1.50)
- [ ] **VICTOIRE by Clare Darcy.** (#E7845—$1.75)
- [ ] **CLANDARA by Evelyn Anthony.** (#E6893—$1.75)
- [ ] **THE FRENCH BRIDE by Evelyn Anthony.**
  (#J7683—$1.95)
- [ ] **MISSION TO MALASPIGA by Evelyn Anthony.**
  (#E6706—$1.75)
- [ ] **THE PERSIAN PRICE by Evelyn Anthony.**
  (#J7254—$1.95)
- [ ] **THE POELLENBERG INHERITANCE by Evelyn Anthony.**
  (#E7838—$1.75)
- [ ] **STRANGER AT THE GATE by Evelyn Anthony.**
  (#W6019—$1.50)
- [ ] **ALYX by Lolah Burford.** (#J7640—$1.95)
- [ ] **MACLYON by Lolah Burford.** (#J7773—$1.95)
- [ ] **MADALENA by Sheila Walsh.** (#W7457—$1.50)
- [ ] **THE GOLDEN SONGBIRD by Sheila Walsh.**
  (#W6639—$1.50)

THE NEW AMERICAN LIBRARY, INC.,
P.O. Box 999, Bergenfield, New Jersey 07621

Please send me the SIGNET BOOKS I have checked above. I am enclosing $_____(check or money order—no currency or C.O.D.'s). Please include the list price plus 35¢ a copy to cover handling and mailing costs. (Prices and numbers are subject to change without notice.)

Name_____

Address_____

City_____State_____Zip Code_____
Allow at least 4 weeks for delivery

The Best in Fiction from SIGNET Books

☐ **DESIRES OF THY HEART** by Joan Carroll Cruz.
(#J7738—$1.95)

☐ **LORD RIVINGTON'S LADY** by Eileen Jackson.
(#W7612—$1.50)

☐ **THE BRACKENROYD INHERITANCE** by Erica Lindley.
(#W6795—$1.50)

☐ **DEVIL IN CRYSTAL** by Erica Lindley. (#E7643—$1.75)

☐ **THE CAPTAIN'S WOMAN** by Mark Logan.
(#J7488—$1.95)

☐ **CONSTANTINE CAY** by Catherine Dillon.
(#E7583—$1.75)

☐ **WHITE FIRES BURNING** by Catherine Dillon.
(#E7351—$1.75)

☐ **THE FIRES OF GLENLOCHY** by Constance Heaven.
(#E7452—$1.75)

☐ **THE PLACE OF STONES** by Constance Heaven.
(#W7046—$1.50)

☐ **HIGHWAYMAN #2: AMOROUS ROGUE** by Raymond Foxall. (#Y7616—$1.25)

☐ **MANNERBY'S LADY** by Sandra Heath.
(#W7492—$1.50)

☐ **THE MASKED HEIRESS** by Vanessa Gray.
(#W7397—$1.50)

☐ **NIGHTINGALE PARK** by Moira Lord. (#E7617—$1.75)

☐ **ROGUE'S MISTRESS** by Constance Gluyas.
(#J7533—$1.95)

☐ **SAVAGE EDEN** by Constance Gluyas. (#J7681—$1.95)

More SIGNET Titles You Will Enjoy

- ☐ **CALDO LARGO by Earl Thompson.** (#E7737—$2.25)
- ☐ **A GARDEN OF SAND by Earl Thompson.**
  (#E8039—$2.50)
- ☐ **TATTOO by Earl Thompson.** (#E8038—$2.50)
- ☐ **THE MANLY-HEARTED WOMAN by Frederick Manfred.**
  (#E7648—$1.75)
- ☐ **THIS IS THE HOUSE by Deborah Hill.**
  (#J7610—$1.95)
- ☐ **TORRENTS by Marie Anne Desmarest.**
  (#E7614—$1.75)
- ☐ **THE DREAM'S ON ME by Dotson Rader.**
  (#E7536—$1.75)
- ☐ **SMOULDERING FIRES by Anya Seton.**
  (#J7276—$1.95)
- ☐ **A FINE ROMANCE by Cynthia Propper Seton.**
  (#W7455—$1.50)
- ☐ **THE HALF-SISTERS by Cynthia Propper Seton.**
  (#W6457—$1.50)
- ☐ **DECADES by Ruth Harris.** (#J6705—$1.95)
- ☐ **ENGAGEMENT by Eloise Weld.** (#E7060—$1.75)
- ☐ **HARVEST OF DESIRE by Rochelle Larkin.**
  (#J7277—$1.95)
- ☐ **LOVE SONG by Adam Kennedy.** (#E7535—$1.75)
- ☐ **THE RESTLESS LADY by Frances Parkinson Keyes.**
  (#E7258—$1.75)

Romance Titles from SIGNET

☐ **BON VOYAGE, MY DARLING by Mary Ann Taylor.**
(#W7554—$1.50)

☐ **CAPTURE MY LOVE by Mary Ann Taylor.**
(#W7755—$1.50)

☐ **FOR LOVE OR MONEY by Vivian Donald.**
(#Y7756—$1.25)

☐ **ENCHANTED JOURNEY by Kristen Michaels.**
(#Y7628—$1.25)

☐ **ENCHANTED TWILIGHT by Kristen Michaels.**
(#Y7733—$1.25)

☐ **A SPECIAL KIND OF LOVE by Kristen Michaels.**
(#Y7039—$1.25)

☐ **SONG OF THE HEART by Kristen Michaels.**
(#W7702—$1.50)

☐ **TO BEGIN WITH LOVE by Kristen Michaels.**
(#Y7732—$1.25)

☐ **IN LOVE'S OWN FASHION by Arlene Hale.**
(#Y6846—$1.25)

☐ **LEGACY OF LOVE by Arlene Hale.** (#W7411—$1.50)

☐ **LOVER'S REUNION by Arlene Hale** (#W7771—$1.50)

☐ **A VOTE FOR LOVE by Arlene Hale.** (#Y7505—$1.25)

☐ **THE SHROUDED WAY by Janet Caird.**
(#Y7665—$1.25)

☐ **A LONG LOST LOVE by Julia Alcott.** (#Y7190—$1.25)

☐ **A SILENT VOICE by Susan Claudia.** (#Q6014—95¢)

THE NEW AMERICAN LIBRARY, INC.,
P.O. Box 999, Bergenfield, New Jersey 07621

Please send me the SIGNET BOOKS I have checked above. I am
enclosing $_____(check or money order—no currency
or C.O.D.'s). Please include the list price plus 35¢ a copy to cover
handling and mailing costs. (Prices and numbers are subject to
change without notice.)

Name_____

Address_____

City_____State_____Zip Code_____
Allow at least 4 weeks for delivery